Witch Is When Stuff Got Serious

Chapter 1

There was an attractive young woman with long, blonde hair, sitting behind Mrs V's desk. Before I could ask her what she was doing there, *she* addressed *me*.

"Good morning, Madam. Welcome to the offices of Ken Gooder, Private Investigator. How may I help you this morning?"

I was obviously missing something. "Jill Gooder," I said.

"Miss Gooder isn't in at the moment. Do you have an appointment?"

"No. *I'm* Jill Gooder."

"Oh! Sorry, I didn't recognise you. You looked different on Skype."

I was beginning to get bad vibes.

"Could you remind me—when exactly was it we talked on Skype?"

"You interviewed me for this job. Remember?"

"Of course. And when was that, again?"

"A couple of days ago. You said I was just what you were looking for, and that I could start immediately."

"Oh yes. Silly me. It must have slipped my mind. I'm sorry, but I've also forgotten your name?"

"Julie Rules. But everyone calls me Jules."

"Right. So, Jules Rules?"

"That's right."

"Remind me again, Jules. What experience have you had as a PA?"

"Like I said in the interview, I've been working in a black pudding factory."

"As a PA?"

"No. Packing black puddings."

"Have you done any other work, apart from packing black puddings?"

"Oh yes. I packed sausages for a little while. But then they promoted me."

"To black puddings?"

"That's right."

"I guess this is going to be quite a change for you, isn't it?"

"Yes. I'm really excited. I know it's only temporary, but I feel like once I've got this on my CV, it will open other doors for me."

"I guess so. Do you have much experience with computers?"

"Not much. I've got a smartphone though."

"Right."

"And a tablet."

"That's nice. I'd better go through to my office. You carry on doing — err — whatever it is you're doing."

"Okay, Miss Gooder."

"Call me Jill."

"Okay, Jill. Would you like me to make you a cup of tea?"

"Yeah, that would be nice. One and two thirds spoonfuls of sugar please."

She looked a little worried. "I'm not very good with decimals."

"Never mind. Just make the tea, and I'll put my own sugar in."

"Okay then."

"Winky! Where are you, Winky?"

He came crawling out from under my desk. "You called?"

"What have you done?"

"Nothing. I was asleep."

"I mean little Miss Black Pudding out there?"

"Pretty isn't she?"

"Yes, she's very pretty."

"Beautiful hair."

"Yes, yes, but what's she doing sitting at Mrs V's desk?"

"The last time I looked, she was filing her nails."

"Why does she think she's my new temp?"

"She *is* your new temp. I gave her the job."

"You can't go around recruiting people!"

"You should thank me. You said that you were too busy to do it yourself."

"She has no experience."

"She's packed black puddings."

"Yeah, and sausages. But that's hardly relevant. She's barely even used a computer."

"It's not like the old bag lady was much use. She just sat there all day knitting or crocheting or whatever it is she did with those needles. I can't see how Jules will be any worse."

"Do you take milk?" Jules' voice came through the intercom—making both me and Winky jump. I'd almost forgotten I had an intercom; Mrs V never used it because she was too hard of hearing. "Miss Gooder? Do you take milk?"

I pressed the 'speak' button. "Yes Jules. Just a drop, please."

"Okay, I'll bring it through."

I turned back to Winky. "Exactly what made you choose Jules as my new temp?"

He thought about it for a moment. "Two things actually.

First, she's very easy on the eye."

"That's hardly a qualification for the job."

"And, secondly, she loves cats."

"I should have known."

"Here you are, Miss Gooder." Jules came in, carrying a cup of tea. "Whoops! I've spilt a bit. Do you have a cloth?"

"It's okay, Jules. I'll see to it."

"Oh look! Your cat's come out. He's so cute, isn't he? I love cats. Don't you, Miss Gooder?"

"*Please* call me Jill."

"Okay, Jill. What's his name?"

"This is Winky."

"Why do you call him that?"

"Because of his eyes?"

"What about them?"

Oh boy.

"He's only got one."

"Oh yeah! I see. Winky, yeah. That's funny. I've got four cats."

"Really?"

"They're my mum's actually. I still live with my parents. I collect cat ornaments too. And jewellery—look!" She pointed to a small brooch on her lapel. "I've got lots of cat soft toys too. I keep them in my bedroom. I've even got cat wallpaper."

"That's nice. Remind me, where were you when you were interviewed for the job?"

"In my bedroom."

"I see. And that's where the cat wallpaper and soft toys are?"

"Yes."

It was all starting to make sense.

"Thanks, Jules."

She turned to walk away, but then stopped. "Oh, by the way, Jill. I did what you asked, on my way into work."

"You did? Good. What was that, again?"

"I bought some salmon, red not pink. And full cream milk. The salmon is in the cupboard, and the milk's in the fridge. But I'll need the money otherwise I won't have the bus fare home."

"Don't worry. I'll make sure you get your money before you leave."

"Thanks. Is there anything else you need me to do?"

"Not at the moment. Just answer the phone if anybody calls, but please don't say 'Ken Gooder'."

"But that's what the sign outside says?"

"Yes, I know. I haven't actually got around to changing it, yet. If you could say, 'Jill Gooder, P.I.', that would be great."

"Okay. It's a little bit confusing though, isn't it?"

"I'm sure you'll get the hang of it."

"There is one more thing, Jill. There seems to be a lot of scarves in the cupboard and desk drawers. Quite a lot of socks, too. Am I meant to be doing something with those?"

"No, you don't need to worry about them. They belong to Mrs V, my regular PA/receptionist. She knits a lot."

"I wish I could knit. I tried once, but I couldn't understand it."

"It can be complicated. Do you have any other hobbies, Jules?"

"Mainly YouTube. And Facebook. And a bit of Instagram. And collecting cat soft toys, of course."

"Of course. Okay, well off you go. I'll catch up with you

later."

"Okay, Jill. Thanks!"

I turned to Winky. "I hope you didn't tell Jules I was going to pay her."

"Of course you have to pay her. You don't think she's going to work for nothing, do you?"

"Great, so I have to pay her, even though she's had no experience whatsoever, and doesn't know how to use a computer?"

"She's very good with cats though."

***

"I'm getting a drum kit for my birthday, Auntie Jill!" Mikey was on at me as soon as I walked through Kathy's front door.

"So I hear."

"I can't bring it home because Mum and Dad say it will be too noisy, but I can play it at Tom Tom every day."

"Not *every* day." Kathy rolled her eyes. "Do you remember what we agreed?"

"Every day except Monday?"

"Two days a week."

"Aw, but Mum. That's not much."

"It's either that or no drum kit. Okay?"

"O—kay." Mikey gave an exaggerated sigh.

"I bet Auntie Jill will want to watch you play at Tom Tom. Won't you, Auntie Jill?"

"If I'm not busy. What days will you be going there?"

"Tuesdays and Fridays," Kathy said.

"Tuesdays and Fridays? What a pity. Those are the two days when I have to work late."

"That's lucky then." Kathy grinned. "Because it's actually Mondays and Wednesdays. So, you'll be able to make it." She was so crafty that sister of mine.

"Great. I'll look forward to that."

"Go and wash your hands, Mikey. It's almost time for dinner." Kathy turned to me. "When are you going to bring Jack over for us to meet him?"

"Not yet. I don't want to put him off before we've even started."

"What do you mean, put him off? Are you ashamed of us?"

"No, but I know what you're like. You'll be asking him when the big day is, and how many kids we plan on having."

"So, when is the big day?"

"There is no *big* day. We've only just started seeing one another."

"But you *are seeing* one another, then? As in, *really* seeing one another?"

"I have no idea what that means."

"You know exactly what I mean. Have you had breakfast at his place yet?"

"Stop quizzing her." Peter came out of the living room. "You'll scare her away."

"Not much chance of that. She has almost as many meals here as we do."

"I do not. It's ages since I was around here for dinner."

"What about last Monday?"

"Yeah, but before that."

"Friday. And Wednesday."

"You shouldn't make such delicious meals. Speaking of which — is something burning?"

"Oh no!" Kathy turned tail and headed for the kitchen.

I followed Peter through to the dining room.

"Thanks for rescuing me."

"That's okay. You should tell your sister to mind her own business."

"Do you think that would work?"

"Probably not." He grinned.

An ear-splitting noise came from upstairs.

"What's that?" I clamped my hands over my ears.

Peter mouthed something.

"What?"

He mouthed the word again. "Lizzie."

I lowered my hands, and realised the noise was someone singing — and I use that term loosely — very loosely.

"Winning that talent competition was the worst thing that could have happened." Peter shook his head. "I still don't understand how she did it. She has a terrible voice — even worse than Kathy's, and that's saying something. I had hoped she'd lose, and that would put her off for life. It was like she was possessed that day. Possessed by someone who could actually sing."

Oh bum! Maybe I shouldn't have interfered.

"Lizzie!" Kathy yelled. "Wash your hands and come down. Dinner is almost ready."

"Everything all right in the kitchen?" I asked.

"Yeah. The Yorkshire puddings may be a little well done. Did you hear Lizzie singing?"

"Oh, yes." I heard her.

"We've put her name down for another competition next month. In West Green."

"Are you sure that's a good idea? Wouldn't it be better to quit while she's ahead?"

"And let all that talent go to waste?"

Peter and I exchanged a glance.

"Are you looking forward to the picnic, Auntie Jill?" Lizzie said, through a mouthful of mashed potatoes.

I looked at Kathy who was doing her best not to laugh.

"What picnic is that?"

"We're all going to Sunset Picnic site."

"All?"

"Don't you remember, Auntie Jill?" Kathy said. "You said you wanted to come."

"When was it I said that exactly?"

"Last week. The kids are so pleased you're coming with us."

She'd done it to me again. She knew I couldn't say no when the kids were around. I'd just have to come up with an excuse closer to the time.

Over dinner, I couldn't help but notice that Peter kept mouthing something to Kathy—each time he did it, she shook her head.

"Go on Kathy," he said, eventually. "Tell Jill your news."

"I don't want to tell her. I'm trying to forget about it."

"Trying to forget what? What is it you don't want to tell me?"

"Thanks, Pete." She shot him a look. He'd be in trouble after I'd gone.

"I'm surprised your grandmother hasn't told you."

"Told me *what* for goodness sake?"

"Wool TV approached her a few days ago. They want to do a reality TV show based in Ever."

"That'll make riveting viewing."

"It *will* for viewers of Wool TV—they'll lap it up.

Apparently, it's going to be called Wool Shop Yarns."

"That's a terrible title. Has Grandma agreed to it? I'm surprised she didn't tell them to sling their hook."

"She's really enthusiastic. She sees it as a great opportunity for free publicity, which I suppose it will be. But I'm not keen. I don't want cameramen following me around all day watching me pick my nose."

"Yuk, Mummy!" Lizzie shouted.

"Do you eat it?" Mikey said. "I do."

"Mikey, please!" Peter tapped his son's arm. "Not at the dinner table."

"You might become a TV celebrity." I laughed. The whole idea was hilarious. "You'll get invited on chat shows, and have the paparazzi following you around."

"Don't be ridiculous," Kathy said. "This is Wool TV we're talking about. But what if I make a fool of myself on camera?"

"It will probably end up on YouTube."

"Great! That's all I need. Then the whole world can laugh at me."

"You could open your own channel and monetise it."

"Do what? Since when did you know so much about YouTube?"

"Someone in the office mentioned it the other day."

Chapter 2

Jules came into my office; she looked rather worried.

"Is everything okay?"

"There's a strange woman out there."

"Strange how?"

"Strange altogether. She says you know her daughter."

"Did she tell you her daughter's name?"

"Madeline something?"

"Madeline Lane?"

"Yes, that's her."

I hadn't seen Mad's mother since Mad and I were kids, and to be honest, she used to scare me too, back then.

"Ask her to come in, please, Jules."

Delilah Lane's hair was streaked a dozen different colours. She had a mouth full of gum, and was wearing a skirt which was several years too short for her. The red mascara and green lipstick weren't really working.

"Look at you, Jill. All grown up. I see you managed to grow some boobs eventually."

Did I mention that Mad's mum used to delight in embarrassing me, and all the other kids?

"Hello, Mrs Lane. How are you keeping?"

"Can't complain. Well I could, but nobody wants to know about my varicose veins. Would you like some gum?"

"No, thanks. I'm good."

"What's that ugly looking thing?"

"That's Winky."

He hissed at her.

"I lost my cat, Cleopatra, recently."

"I'm sorry to hear that. How old was she when she died?"

"She isn't dead. I just lost her. I took her to the vets to get her claws clipped, and left her on the bus. I tried lost property, but no one had handed her in. I did get a nice umbrella from there, though."

"What brings you here today, Mrs Lane?"

"It's about time you stopped calling me 'Mrs'. Now you're all grown up. Call me Deli."

"Okay, Deli. What brings you here today?"

"Madeline asked me to come."

"Oh? Where is she?"

"At the police station."

"What's she doing there?"

"Her boss, that snotty-nosed cow with the attitude, got herself murdered last night."

"Murdered?"

"Yeah. Dead as a dodo. Madeline found her after they'd locked up."

"So why is Madeline at the police station?"

"They took her there last night, and she's still there. She said she tried to call you, but couldn't get through, so she called and asked me to pop over here this morning. It's a bit inconvenient really. I'm meant to be having hair extensions put in, but I had to cancel it. It's okay though because Cynthia said she can fit me in tomorrow. So, will you go and see her?"

"Yes. Yes, of course."

"Good, well I'd better get going. I've got fish cakes to buy. Nice to see you again, Jill."

***

Jack Maxwell had been reinstated shortly after he'd

presented Internal Affairs with the digital recording I'd made of Tom Hawk and Craig Beele. Hawk was now facing a number of charges, which would probably land him in prison for several years.

I got through to Jack on the first attempt.

"Jack, it's me."

"Hi, petal."

"What have I told you?"

"About what?" He laughed.

"Don't call me petal."

"It's a term of endearment."

"If you call me that one more time, I'll be forced to break your legs. How's that for endearment? Look, the reason I called is that I've just heard you've got a friend of mine down there. Madeline Lane—she was brought in last night. She works in the library."

"We're still questioning her. She was with the deceased when my people arrived at the library last night."

"Can I see her?"

"Not at the moment. Like I said, we're still interviewing her."

"When then?"

"Some time later today."

"Can I come over there and wait?"

"I'd rather you didn't. I know what you're like. You'll only be in the way. Sorry, I have to go. I'll let you know when we're done with her."

In the way?

"I'm going to the police station, Jules."

"You're not in trouble are you, Jill?"

"No, but I have to go see someone who might be."

"Is there anything you'd like me to do?"

"You could feed Winky in about an hour's time."

"Salmon?"

"No. He's costing me a small fortune. Give him some of that economy tuna, but don't let him see the label. And if the phone rings, you remember what to say?"

"Jill Gooder, private investigator."

"Very good. We'll make a receptionist of you yet."

"Do you really think so?" Her face lit up.

Stranger things have happened.

Life was much simpler when Jack and I had detested one another. Now, we were—err—whatever it was we were—it was much trickier. I couldn't just burst into the police station and demand to see Mad. It would get me nowhere, and would royally cheese off Jack. I'd used invisibility numerous times before to get inside the building, but that wouldn't work this time because Mad would probably be in an interview room or a holding cell. A different approach was needed.

I made my way around the side of the building to the car park. Once there, I waited until there was no one around, then shrank myself, and crawled through one of the vents into the air conditioning ductwork. It was very dark inside there; illuminated only by the light which shone through the grilles along its length. As I crept along, I could see into the various rooms. I had a rough idea where I needed to be, so took a right turn and headed towards what I hoped were the interview rooms.

Suddenly, there was the patter of tiny feet behind me. An enormous spider was rushing my way. I had to act quickly, so I shot a lightning bolt, which hit it square on the nose. That did the trick.

I crawled a little further until I came to the next grille. It was one of the interview rooms, but there was no one in there. I carried on to the next room. In this one, two police officers were interviewing a middle-aged man who was sporting a Mohawk haircut. It really didn't suit him.

There was no one in the first holding cell, but when I looked through the grille into the second one, I saw Mad. She was still dressed in her librarian outfit, but had let her hair down. Seated on a metal bench, she looked thoroughly miserable.

"Mad," I called.

She didn't hear me.

"Mad!" I rattled on the grille.

She looked up at the wall.

"Mad, it's me. Up here."

She looked puzzled, but stood up and walked towards the grille.

"It's Jill. Can you hear me?"

"Jill? What are you doing here?"

"Your mum came to see me. This was the only way I could get to talk to you."

"How on earth did you fit in there?"

"I shrank myself."

"Oh yes. I keep forgetting you can do stuff like that."

"Are you okay?"

"I will be, once they let me out."

"What happened at the library?"

"I honestly don't know. We have the same routine every day at closing time. We lock the main outer doors on the front of the building, and then I take any old books which have been returned, down to the archive. There's usually only a few each day that need to go down there. Normally, by the time I come back upstairs, Anita is ready to leave. She was okay when I left her to go down to the archive, but when I got back upstairs I couldn't see her anywhere. I found her lying behind the desk—in a pool of blood. I checked her pulse, but she was already dead."

"Did you see a murder weapon?"

"There was no sign of one as far as I could see. I don't really know why they're still holding me. I agreed to come in yesterday because I was the only other person at the scene, but they've been questioning me for most of the night, and there's still no sign of them letting me go."

"They'll have to release you soon. Don't worry about it."

"I tried to call you last night, but I couldn't get through, so I rang Mum. I wasn't convinced she'd go and see you. It sounded like it was a lot of bother, to be honest."

"Yeah, she said she'd had to rearrange her hair appointment."

"Oh dear. I'll be in the bad books when I get out."

"It was quite a surprise to see your mother again after all this time."

"She doesn't change much, does she?"

"Not much. She still scares me."

"Did she have Nails with her?"

"Nails? Is that her dog?"

"No, that's her latest fella. His name's actually Simon, but everyone calls him Nails."

"As in 'hard as nails'?"

Mad laughed. "No. As in, he bites his nails all the time. I wouldn't mind if it was just his fingernails."

"Gross!"

"Tell me about it. I daren't eat a pot noodle anywhere

around him, just in case—"

"Don't! You're turning my stomach." No pot noodles for me for the foreseeable future. "Look, I'd better get going. Call me when they release you, and I'll come and pick you up."

***

When I arrived at Cuppy C, the twins were absolutely bubbling with excitement. If past experience was anything to go by, that probably wasn't a good sign.

"Why are you two so hyper?"

"We've had a brilliant idea," Amber said. "And it's one that's going to revolutionise Cuppy C."

That sounded like bad news.

"Don't you remember what happened the last time you tried something new and revolutionary?"

They both looked puzzled.

"The 'deluxe' chocolate fountain?"

"That was different." Pearl waved away my doubts. "This is going to put Cuppy C on the map!"

"And what exactly is 'this'?"

"A conveyor belt." Amber was still bubbling with obvious enthusiasm.

"Sorry? I thought for a moment you said: conveyor belt?"

"That is what I said. Brilliant, eh?"

"A conveyor belt?"

"Yep."

"In here?"

"Yep."

"Just one question?"

"Go on." Pearl was every bit as enthusiastic as her sister.

"Have you lost your tiny minds?"

Their faces fell—that obviously wasn't the reaction they'd been hoping for.

"It's a great idea!" Amber didn't try to hide her annoyance.

"You don't understand the food service industry." Pearl appeared equally put out.

"I *have* seen a conveyor belt in a sushi bar," I conceded.

"Well then," Amber said. "There you are."

"But I'm not sure it will work in here. I've never heard of a tea room with a conveyor belt."

"That's the whole point!" Amber was enthused again. "We'll be the first."

"Pioneers!" Pearl beamed.

"So how exactly will it work?"

"The buns and cakes will go around and around the tea room." Amber waved her hand in a circular motion to illustrate the principle. "People can take whatever they fancy from the conveyor, and then pay for it when they leave the shop."

"And what's even better," Pearl said. "Is when customers see our cakes going by their table, they won't be able to resist them. Sales will triple!"

"Whatever gave you the idea for this?"

"A man came into the shop a couple of days ago. He told us all about it."

"A man? It wasn't the same man who sold you the chocolate fountain, was it?"

"No." Pearl turned to Amber. "It wasn't, was it?"

"No. This man had a moustache and a beard."

Hmm?

"Did he actually show you any pictures of other tea rooms

that have successfully implemented the conveyor belt?"

"You're missing the point, Jill," Amber said. "We'll be the first."

"I'm not sure that's a good thing. It sounds like he'll be using Cuppy C as a test bed."

"Jill, you simply don't understand the tea room business."

"Apparently not."

Chapter 3

Mr Ivers had a real spring in his step. Whatever did he have to be so happy about? I thought he'd still be in mourning over his Diamond. When he'd found out how much it would cost to have the correct engine fitted, he'd been forced to sell it.

"Morning, Jill! Isn't it a beautiful day?"

"Gorgeous, yes. Pity you can't take a run out in the Diamond." Sometimes, it was scary how cruel I could be.

"That's life, I guess. No good crying over spilled cream."

"Milk."

"Sorry?"

"Never mind. So, why are you so chipper? Are there some blockbuster movies out this week?"

"I haven't had time to think about the movies. I've had other things on my mind."

I could sense he was dying for me to ask, but I'm not that stupid.

"Funny you should ask," he said.

Huh?

"I've met a lovely young woman."

"Really?"

"Yes, through Love Spell."

I was surprised the Love Spell girls hadn't kicked him off their books. According to Hilary, all the witches he'd dated up until now had said he was boring—big surprise!

"That's nice. Have you had many dates with her?"

"No. We've only been out on the one."

That figured.

"But we really clicked—right from the get go. Her name's Tess. She's lovely."

"Does she like the cinema, too?"

"No, funnily enough she doesn't. And yet, it doesn't bother me. In fact, I've barely thought about movies since I met her. I only just managed to get this week's column for The Bugle completed on time."

"Wow. It sounds like Tess has really made an impression on you."

"She certainly has."

"I'm very pleased for you, Mr Ivers. That's great news."

"I can't wait for you to meet her. I'm sure you'll like her."

If Tess could keep Ivers off my back, then I was sure I would.

***

It was late afternoon, and I was thinking about calling it a day when the phone rang. It was Mad.

"Jill, they've just released me. Are you still okay to come and pick me up?"

"Sure, no problem. Stay where you are. I'll be with you in a few minutes."

I jumped in the car, and drove over to the police station. Mad was waiting for me in reception.

"Are you okay?"

"Yeah. Just tired. I need a shower and some shut-eye."

"Come on, then. I'll get you home. Or you can stay at my place if you'd prefer?"

"No. It's okay, Jill. I'd rather get back home."

We were about to leave the building when Jack Maxwell appeared.

"Jill, wait a minute, please." He had another officer by his side.

"What's up, Jack?"

"Madeline Lane, I'm arresting you for the murder of Anita Pick." The other officer took Mad's arm, and led her back inside the station. She was too tired and shocked to resist.

"What's going on?"

"Sorry." Jack pulled me to one side.

"What on earth are you playing at? You've only just released her. Why are you charging her?"

"We've found the murder weapon. It was on one of the bookshelves in the library. The fingerprints on it belong to your friend."

***

Late afternoon, the next day, my phone rang. It was Pearl. She was so excited she could barely get the words out.

"Jill! You have to come over now! Come and see the conveyor belt!"

Cuppy C had been closed all morning for the engineers to install it. I'd tried several times to warn the twins that I didn't think it was a good idea, but they were adamant that it would put them ahead of the competition.

"Will you come over, Jill? Please! You've got to see this!"

"Okay, I'm on my way."

"It's brilliant, isn't it?" Amber looked like a young child on Christmas morning.

The conveyor belt started behind the counter, went over to the wall, ran along that wall and the next, and then cut through the middle of the shop, back to the counter.

"It's very long." I observed.

"It had to be long," Amber said. "To cover all of the

tables."

"Yeah, I can see that. But how do people get from that side of the shop to the other? The conveyor belt cuts them off."

"They have to duck underneath it."

"Right. Of course. Why didn't I think of that?"

"Would you like to see a demo?" Pearl said.

"Sure. Why not?"

"Sit over there, then." Pearl pointed. "At the table against the far wall."

Once I was seated, Amber and Pearl started to load the conveyor belt with a selection of cakes and buns. I was rather peckish, and quite fancied a blueberry muffin. Once the cakes were on the conveyor belt, one of the twins pressed the start button, and it began to move. Slowly — *very* slowly. Almost as slow as Mr Ivers' Diamond.

By the time my blueberry muffin made its way around the shop, I would have starved to death. It would have been quicker to go and fetch one from the bakery.

"It's a bit slow, isn't it, girls?"

"Have some patience, Jill. There's probably a way to make it go quicker. We just need time to work it out."

"Okay. In the meantime, I think I'll just walk over here and get my muffin because by the time it reaches me, it'll be past its sell by date."

***

It was two days since Mad had been arrested. She'd been charged with the murder of Anita Pick, and was being held on remand at Longdale Prison, which was a thirty-mile drive from Washbridge. I'd been in touch with her mother who had managed to arrange a pass for me to visit

Mad.

Longdale was a depressing place. I joined the queue of relatives and friends who were waiting to visit their loved ones. After a quick pat down, we were allowed into the waiting area. Then, five minutes later, a bell rang, and we were ushered through to a much larger room where the inmates were already seated at tables. I spotted Mad in the far corner of the room. She looked tired and drawn—not her usual bubbly self at all.

"How are you?" It was a stupid question.

"I've been better."

"I'm going to help you get out of here, but I need you to take me through exactly what happened that day."

"Like I told you before, Anita was fine when we locked up. I went down to the archive, and when I got back, she was dead. I can't have been gone for more than ten minutes—fifteen at the most."

"Are you absolutely sure the library was empty when you locked up?"

"As sure as I can be. We have the same routine every day. The two of us walk through the library just before closing time, to hurry along any stragglers. Normally, by then, there's no more than half a dozen people still inside. Once we've seen the last few out, we lock up."

"What happened after you found her?"

"I called the ambulance and the police. I don't really know why I bothered with the ambulance because I knew Anita was dead. Once the police arrived, I unlocked the doors, and let them in. The paramedics arrived shortly after."

"Had you seen anyone acting suspiciously during the day?"

"No, but to be honest, I'd spent most of the time hiding in

the cupboard—the one you found me in the other day."

"Getting in some target practice with the crossbow?"

"No. Catching up on my sleep. We'd been to a function, sponsored by the Carnation Foundation, the night before. Anita and me were both invited. I didn't really want to go, but I didn't have much say in the matter. I may have had a couple of drinks too many, so the next day, I was still pretty much out on my feet. Anita didn't seem to care that I'd gone AWOL; I think she'd pretty much given up on me."

"Did Anita ever mention anyone who might have wanted to hurt her?"

"We didn't talk much. She didn't like me, and if I'm honest, I didn't like her very much either. We exchanged pleasantries each morning and evening, but that was about it. She moaned about her ex-husband a lot. I don't know much about him, but from what I can gather, they were going through a rather messy divorce. The only other thing that comes to mind is that she had an ongoing dispute with her next door neighbour. I don't know what it was about—dogs or something, I think. It sounded like a storm in a teacup to me, but her neighbour came into the library a few times. The two of them had a shouting match once. I had to intervene, and escort her neighbour off the premises because it was getting a bit heated."

***

Great! Just what I needed!

I was on my way home after visiting Mad in prison when my car decided to give up on me.

I hated cars.

I managed to pull into a lay-by on a quiet country road, but when I took out my phone to call roadside assistance, the battery was stone dead. Fantastic! Could this day get any better?

Parked a hundred metres in front of me, in the same lay-by, was a white van. Maybe the owner would let me use his phone? As I walked towards it, I passed an A-board which read: *'Malcom the Mobile Barber'*.

Inside the van was a man wearing a flat cap; he was fast asleep with his head on the steering wheel. When I knocked on the window, he stirred, and opened the door.

"Sorry, my dear, I only do men's hair."

"I'm not actually after a haircut. I'm parked back there. My car's broken down and my phone is dead. I wondered if you had a phone I could use?"

"Yes, of course, dear. Come on board."

Once I was inside, I could see he'd removed all the seats from what had obviously once been a minibus, and turned it into a small barber's shop, complete with mirror, sink and barber's chair. I'd never seen anything quite like it.

Roadside assistance confirmed my call was important to them, which was nice to know, and then put me on hold for fifteen minutes. When I eventually managed to speak to someone, they told me a mechanic would be with me as soon as possible—whatever that meant.

"I've never seen a mobile barber's van like this one before," I said.

"This little beauty is a one-off." He was obviously proud of his mobile workplace.

"I'm Jill. I assume you're Malcolm."

"None other."

I hadn't seen more than a dozen cars go by since I'd pulled over.

"Do you get much trade out here, Malcolm?"

"Oh, yes. I've had two customers already."

"Today?"

"No." He laughed.

"This week?"

"This month."

"Two this month? That's not many is it?"

"Then there's my regulars."

"Right. And do you have many regulars?"

"Oh yes. There's Bill."

"Bill?"

"Yes, and Timothy."

"Two then?"

"But Timothy has shaved his head for charity, so he probably won't need my services for a while."

"Have you ever considered parking somewhere a little busier? Maybe closer to the town centre?"

"No, dear. Too much competition there. Out here I've got it all to myself."

I sat and chatted with Malcolm for the next thirty minutes. He was obviously completely bonkers, but appeared perfectly happy to ply his trade in the middle of nowhere. It was already halfway through the month, so by my calculations he was probably doing one haircut per week. It made my business look like a thriving concern.

I was glad to see the mechanic arrive, and even more pleased it wasn't the same man who'd come out to Mr Ivers' Diamond. This guy found a loose connection on the alternator. At least, that's what he told me—it meant nothing to me.

I waved to Malcolm as I sped off, but he already had his head back on the steering wheel.

Chapter 4

As I walked along the street, I noticed there were several large vans parked directly outside of Ever A Wool Moment. Surely, they couldn't all be making deliveries? When I got closer, I spotted the Wool TV logo on the side of the vehicles. Of course! They must be setting up for the reality TV show that Kathy had mentioned. I was curious to see what was happening, so I went inside and found Kathy sitting in a chair behind the counter. A young woman was doing her make-up.

"How's it going, Kathy?"

"I'm fed up already." She certainly looked it. "I have to wear this stupid mic all the time, and the cameras are going to be following me no matter where I go."

"Not to the loo, surely?"

"No, Jill. Not to the loo."

"How long are they going to be here?"

"Every day this week."

Suddenly, Grandma appeared from the back office. She was dressed to the nines.

"Are you going to a wedding, Grandma?" I quipped. She gave me a look.

"I always dress like this, Jill. You know that." Then she turned to Kathy. "I'll walk the floor today as usual."

Kathy rolled her eyes. "She doesn't normally show her face out here for more than a few minutes each day," she whispered. "She usually hides herself away in the back, and leaves muggins here to do everything. She's just desperate to get herself on TV."

"Young man," Grandma shouted at the director. "Don't forget to include close-ups of the displays of Everlasting

Wool and One-Size Knitting Needles."

"I'll do my best."

"You better had. I'm doing you a favour allowing your cameras in here."

"Will this be going out live?" I asked.

The director was obviously pleased to escape from Grandma's interrogation. "Yes, we'll be carrying a live stream throughout the day with a highlights program each evening."

"Is there a time delay on the live stream? In case anything goes wrong?"

"No. It's completely live — warts and all."

Speaking of warts. How come Grandma's wart had disappeared?

"Why are you staring at me, Jill?" she said.

Whoops.

"Err — I was — err nothing."

Either she'd found the world's best concealer or magic was involved. Maybe it would work on my frown lines?

"Okay, everyone!" The director shouted. "We go live in three, two — "

That was my cue to leave. I had a feeling that the next week could turn out to be very entertaining indeed.

***

When I arrived at Aunt Lucy's, I found her staring out of the window, tutting to herself. She hadn't even noticed me walk into the room.

"Ahem!"

"Oh. Hello, Jill. I didn't hear you come in."

"Is anything wrong, Aunt Lucy?"

"Look at the state of this garden. It's a real mess."

"Hasn't Sebastian been around lately?"

"I had to sack him."

"Why?"

"Come on, Jill. You don't have to pretend. I know what happened between him and the twins."

"They told you?"

"They didn't volunteer the information, but I'm their mother—I know when something's wrong. I got it out of them eventually. Stupid girls. I sat them down and gave them a serious talking to. They've got two lovely fiancés, and yet they spend their time flirting with the gardener. Ridiculous! And, it's left me in the lurch—I could hardly keep Sebastian on after that debacle. Look at my rhododendrons. I've never seen them looking so sorry for themselves."

Now, I understood why the twins had suddenly rediscovered their fiancés, and had started house-hunting. Aunt Lucy must have given them a real dressing-down. The garden still looked quite splendid—it put mine to shame. But Aunt Lucy's standards were extremely high, and I could see she was upset.

"I don't suppose you know any gardeners, do you, Jill?"

"I know one—my brother-in-law, Peter, but I can't exactly ask him. He's a human, so he can't come to Candlefield."

"That's a pity. I think I'm going to have to put an advert in The Candle."

"What about Lester? Does he do any gardening?"

"Lester? Goodness, no. I wouldn't trust him with my garden. I love the man to bits, but I don't think he'd know a hydrangea from a hyena."

"Talking of Lester, are you and he still thinking of moving

to the human world?"

I had my fingers crossed that she'd dropped the idea of moving in with me.

"Lester suggested we could rent some sort of weekend retreat over in Washbridge, so we could see how I adjust."

"That sounds like a great idea."

"I'm just going to see how things develop. I'm not in any great hurry, I must admit."

"Aunt Lucy, while I'm here, there's something I wanted to talk to you about."

"What's that, dear?"

"It's a bit of a confession, actually."

"Oh?" She looked a little concerned.

"I've met my father."

"But I thought you said you didn't want to see him?"

"I hadn't planned to, but I literally bumped into him in Washbridge."

"Hmm? That probably wasn't a coincidence."

"I did wonder about that, but anyway we've met up again since then. He seemed very worried about my safety, and kept warning me to be careful."

"Are you going to keep seeing him?"

"No. I have nothing to say to him. He abandoned me for no apparent reason, and made no effort to see me again. He's not a part of my life. I have my family here in Candlefield, and my family in Washbridge. I don't need him."

"Good. It's probably for the best."

"Is Grandma still seeing Horace?"

"Yes, as far as I know."

"What do you think of him?"

"He's a strange man. I don't really know what to make of

him."

"To be honest, he gives me the creeps. He came to my flat."

"With Grandma?"

"No, by himself."

"Why?"

"I don't know, but he seems to know all about my sister and her family."

"Have you mentioned this to Grandma?"

"No."

"You should."

"What would I say? *'Your new boyfriend gives me the creeps'*? Maybe I just need time to get to know him."

***

I'd tried really hard to persuade the twins that they should have a 'soft' launch of the conveyor belt—to test it while there weren't many people in the shop, so they could iron out all of the problems. But no—they knew best. They wanted a big launch party, and they'd invited everyone.

And, today was the day.

Everyone who was anyone in Candlefield was in Cuppy C, including the mayor, the chief of police, numerous level six witches, and reporters from The Candle. Aunt Lucy and Lester were there too, along with the twins' fiancés. Grandma had cried off; she said she had important business in Washbridge. I had a feeling she had a sense of what was to come. I'd thought I was there as a guest too, but it turned out they wanted me to work behind the counter. Great. I'd got all dressed up for nothing.

Amber and Pearl had both invested heavily in new outfits, and they'd spent hours preparing a speech which went on for way too long. Everyone in the audience looked comatose by the time Pearl wrapped it up.

"And so, in closing," she said. "It is with great pleasure that we switch on the first tea room conveyor belt in Candlefield." Both of them placed a hand on the red button, and pressed.

Just like before, the conveyor belt set off at a snail's pace. If anything, it was even slower, probably because of the number of cakes which had been piled onto it. After a few minutes, the cakes were still making their way slowly around the room. The guests were becoming more and more impatient. The rumbles of complaint got louder as people grew tired of waiting for their cake.

"I thought you'd sorted this?" I said.

"We did." Amber looked stressed. "We got it going faster, but I can't remember how we did it." She pressed a button, and the conveyor belt started to go in reverse. There were more moans and groans as the cakes got even further away from the guests. She pressed a different button, which at least meant it was travelling in the right direction again.

Pearl pulled one of the levers. "I think it's this," she said.

"No. It isn't." Amber pulled it back.

"Yes it is."

"No, it's not."

Suddenly, the lever broke off in their hands, and the conveyor belt began to speed around the room so quickly that the cakes flew off in all directions. A custard tart hit the mayor smack bang in the face. Buns were spilling into people's laps.

Amber jumped up onto the counter and shouted, "Don't panic. Everything's in hand."

But it was way too late; everyone was leaving. The last person to leave the shop was the photographer from The Candle. He turned, and snapped a few photos.

I could already picture the next morning's headlines.

***

Everyone else had left, but I stayed on in Cuppy C. It seemed a shame to let the blueberry muffins go to waste.

"Hi, Jill." It was Annie Christy. "Where is everyone? And what's that monstrous thing?"

"A conveyor belt. It's the twins' latest brainwave, but things didn't quite go to plan."

"Oh dear. Can you spare me a minute?"

"Sure. Would you like a drink?"

"No, I can't stay. I popped in on the off chance that I'd catch you here. I know you're never far away from the blueberry muffins."

Harsh, but true.

Some time ago, I'd been hired to find out who was sabotaging Annie's mother's bakery business. It turned out that it was actually her mother who was behind it. She'd done it for the best of reasons. Annie had wanted her to sell the business and retire, but her mother had been dead set against the idea. She hadn't known how to tell her daughter that she didn't want to sell up and retire, so she'd sabotaged her own business to put off the potential buyer. Anyway, it had all ended well, and afterwards, Annie and SupAid had helped me to find an expert for Lester to consult when he temporarily lost his magic powers.

"I haven't seen you for ages, Annie. How are things at SupAid?"

"Not great, actually. That's the reason I'm here. I'm after a favour. I'll get straight to the point, Jill. Donations to SupAid are at an all-time low. I'm not sure why. Money's tight, I guess. We're struggling to meet our commitments. What we need is a big fundraiser—something that will really make an impact, and replenish the coffers. The truth is that myself and my colleagues are all out of ideas. I wondered if maybe you could come up with some suggestions?"

"Me? I know nothing about fundraising. What made you think of me?"

"You have the highest profile of all the witches in Candlefield, so anything you do will probably get the headlines."

"But I wouldn't know where to start."

"Will you at least think about it?"

"Yes, of course. If I come up with anything, I'll give you a call."

"Thanks, Jill. That's all I can ask. I'd better be off. I've got an appointment in five minutes. Nice to see you again."

A fundraiser? That sort of thing was more Kathy's department. She was always raising funds for the school or some other good cause. I could just imagine how that conversation would go.

"Hey, Kathy. Do you have any suggestions for a fundraiser?"

"What's it for?"

"SupAid."

"Never heard of it."

"They help supernatural creatures who have temporarily lost their magical powers."

"Do what?"
"You know. Witches, wizards — that sort of thing."
"Have you been drinking again, Jill?"

Chapter 5

I was pleased to discover that the mini-market across the road from my block of flats had, at long last, restocked on custard creams. And about time, too!

Jammie Dodgers, indeed!

I bought five packets—just in case there was a rush on them.

There was a large crowd gathered around the front of my building. What was going on? As I got closer, I noticed a number of small signs which had been pushed into the grass. They read: *'Yard Sale Today'*.

I enjoyed a good yard sale. Obviously, most of what was on offer was usually rubbish, but you could occasionally pick up a bargain. This one had certainly attracted a crowd; there were dozens of people milling around. It was only when I got closer that I realised the person running the yard sale was none other than Betty Longbottom.

My heart sank.

I took a quick look around the tables, and sure enough, there was all the contraband which she'd had stashed in her spare bedroom. The contraband which I'd managed to hide from the police when they'd caught her shoplifting. I'd made her promise that she'd return all of these goods, and stop the shoplifting. So why was she selling it in a yard sale?

"Betty!"

"Hi, Jill."

"Or should I call you Miss Longbottom?"

"Betty's fine. I only insist on Miss Longbottom when I'm on duty."

"I thought tax inspectors were always on duty. Did Luther get in touch with you?"

"He did. Everything is sorted now. Nothing for you to worry about."

"Good."

I would have loved to be a fly on the wall when Betty met Luther. She'd probably thrown herself at him. Poor old Luther — having to fight off a rampant Longbottom.

"Hi, Jill."

Speak of the devil.

"Hi, gorgeous." Luther planted a kiss on Betty's lips.

What? How? Why?

"Morning, Luthie." Betty was positively glowing.

Luthie?

Was this some kind of practical joke? Had they staged this little charade for my benefit?

"Are you two — err — I mean — are you?" My brain had turned to mush.

"We are!" Betty gushed. "And it's all thanks to you!"

"Yes. Thanks, Jill." Luther flashed that sexy smile of his.

How had Betty Longbottom gone from Norman AKA Mastermind to sex god, Luther Stone?

"I've got to dash, Betty." Luther planted another kiss on her lips. "Bye, Jill."

I was still too stunned to speak.

"Don't you think he's sexy?" Betty said, once he'd left.

"I suppose. Can't say I'd really thought about it."

"Do you see anything you'd like to buy, Jill?"

She was doing a brisk trade, but that was hardly surprising. There were designer shoes, dresses, coats and handbags. Plus, jewellery and expensive perfume. All at rock-bottom prices.

"No, there *isn't* anything I want to buy. What do you think you're doing selling this stuff?"

"It's taking up room in my flat."

"You promised me you'd take it all back to the shops."

"I know, but it would have taken too long. I thought the best thing I could do would be to sell it, and give the proceeds to charity."

That was something, at least.

"Which charity?"

"Crustaceans Rescue And Preservation."

"C.R.A.P?"

"Yes."

You couldn't make this stuff up.

***

A brand new bar had opened in Washbridge, so I decided to check it out. It was called Bar Fish, which I thought was an unusual choice of name, but when I walked inside I could see why. One whole wall was a gigantic fish tank filled with every size and shape of tropical fish imaginable. I was absolutely mesmerised. But it didn't end there. Glass tubes ran along the walls, and below my feet were large tanks which ran the full length of the building. It was amazing!

The barman greeted me with a smile.

"This place is spectacular," I said.

"It is kind of amazing, isn't it?" The man's waistcoat was covered in pictures of tropical fish.

"Could I have a small, white wine, please?"

"I'm sorry, madam. We only serve fishtails."

"Fishtails?"

"It's our version of a cocktail."

"Oh, right. I see. Could I have the drinks list, then."

Every drink was named after a tropical fish. "What would you recommend?"

"The Silver Shark is very nice. It's not too strong for this time of day."

"Okay, then. I'll give it a try."

Once I had my drink, I found a table close to the wall of fish. The fishtail was a little bitter, but perfectly acceptable.

"Jill!" a familiar voice said.

"Mr Ivers?"

"What do you think of this place?" he said. "Brilliant, isn't it?"

"Absolutely. I can't stay long, though. I have a meeting." I thought I'd better get my excuses in early before he decided to join me.

"You must stay long enough to meet Tess."

"Is she here?"

"Yes. She's just popped to the loo." He glanced around. "There she is now."

I followed his gaze.

Oh no! Tess—I should have realised. It was Alicia.

"Tess." Mr Ivers beamed. "This is Jill. She lives in the same block of flats as me."

Tess, or Alicia, or whatever she was calling herself today, flashed me her evil smile, and held out her hand. "So pleased to meet you, Jill. I've heard so much about you."

"Likewise."

Our handshake was brutal; neither of us gave an inch.

"I'm just going to pop to the loo myself," Mr Ivers said. "And then we have to get going."

"What are you playing at, Alicia?" I said, as soon as he was out of earshot.

"Who, me? Nothing."

"Don't give me that. Do you expect me to believe it's a coincidence that you're dating my neighbour?"

"You know how much I love humans."

"If you harm Mr Ivers, you'll have me to answer to."

"You don't scare me, Gooder. Provided the human keeps me amused, he'll be fine. But if he bores me, well —"

"I'm back." Mr Ivers was all smiles. "I hope you two weren't talking about me."

"I think Jill may be a little jealous." Alicia gave him a kiss on the cheek.

Mr Ivers blushed. "Come on, Tess. Let's make tracks. We can go and have another look at those dresses you saw earlier."

That woman was pure evil.

***

The twins were once again with their fiancés in Cuppy C. I'd never seen them spend so much time together. They were all seated at the same window table while a couple of their assistants were behind the counter.

At least, now the conveyor belt had been dismantled and taken away, I could get to them without having to crawl along the floor.

"Hi, guys."

They all greeted me warmly.

"I see you got rid of the conveyor belt."

"Good riddance!" Pearl said. "Amber and her bright ideas."

"It wasn't *my* idea!" Amber rounded on her sister. "It was yours."

"Wasn't!"

"Was!"

William rolled his eyes. Alan shook his head.

"Well, it's gone now." I interrupted. "That's the main thing. Anyway, it's nice to see you two spending time with your fiancés."

"I don't know why we bothered," Amber said. "All these two want to talk about is BoundBall."

"Boring!" Pearl faked a yawn.

Alan and William looked suitably chastised, but only for the briefest of moments. Then they went back to their conversation.

I'd been a guest of honour at the last BoundBall competition by way of thanks for finding the missing trophy. It had been a hugely popular event which had drawn a massive crowd.

Bingo! I'd had an idea.

"Can I join you for a few minutes?"

"Of course, pull up a chair."

"Annie Christy came to see me."

"How is she? And how's her mum?"

"Fine, but Annie's worried about SupAid. They're struggling for donations. She asked if I could come up with any ideas for a fundraising event."

"Have you thought of anything?" Amber said.

"I hadn't, but I have now. What about if the women take on the men at BoundBall?"

Suddenly Alan and William looked up, and both began to laugh—hysterically.

"What's so funny about that?" I didn't bother trying to

hide my annoyance at their reaction.

"Women?" Alan managed through his laughter. "Play BoundBall?"

"That's a joke, right?" William said.

"Why shouldn't women play BoundBall?"

"They never have. It's a man's sport," William said.

I could feel my anger rising. *A man's sport?*

"Okay, you two, so if I could organise this, I assume you'd be willing to give the women's team a start?"

"We could give them a hundred start," William said. "They'd still have no chance."

"Right, you're on. I'll make the arrangements with Annie Christy. We'll sort out a day and a venue, and we'll whoop your asses."

"Of course you will." They both laughed.

"Anyway, we'd better be making tracks," William said. "We'll leave you women to come up with a game plan. You're going to need one."

Alan and William were still laughing as they made their way out of the tea room. After they'd left, Amber and Pearl turned to me. They looked horrified.

"What were you thinking, Jill?" Amber said. "Women can't take on the men at BoundBall, we'll get slaughtered!"

"Of course we can. If they give us a hundred start, how difficult can it be?"

"Where are you going to get a team from?"

"I don't know. I'll put an advert in The Candle, and I can stick a flyer on your notice board. I'm sure it won't be that difficult to assemble a team of women to take on the men. Let's show them what we're made of."

"What do you mean, *we*?" Amber said. "*I'm* not playing."

"Nor me," Pearl said. "I've never played BoundBall."

"Come on, girls, surely you're not going to let me down?"

"You're on your own, Jill. Best of luck."

I called Annie Christy to give her the good news.

"Annie, I've think I've come up with an idea."

"Really? What is it?"

"I thought we could organise a BoundBall match—men versus women."

She went silent, and for a moment, I thought we'd been cut off.

"Annie, are you there?"

"Are you insane, Jill?"

Not quite the reaction I'd hoped for.

"No. I think it could work. It should stir up some interest."

"Oh, it'll definitely do that. Every man in Candlefield will be there to laugh at your team."

"I don't care. If it raises money, what does it matter? And besides which, they said we could have a hundred start. With that, I think we have a good chance of winning."

"Okay, Jill. I'm happy to go along with it if you're willing to organise a team."

"Of course I am."

"Okay then. We'll talk again soon. Bye."

Oh, bum! What had I let myself in for now?

***

I didn't go shopping with Kathy very often because she usually ended up driving me insane. She could spend forever looking at shoes or handbags, and still end up buying nothing. Today though, she'd persuaded me to help her pick out some new curtains. As she'd rightly pointed out, I had impeccable taste when it came to soft furnishings.

We'd just come out of 'It's Curtains For You', when I heard someone call my name. I didn't recognise the woman at first, but then, when she got closer, I realised it was Dorothy's mother, Dolly.

"Hello there, Dolly. What brings you to Washbridge?"

"I'm here to see how Dorothy is settling in."

"How is she doing?"

"Very well, thank you. And it's all down to you. It was great what you did—helping her to find that apartment. She really fell on her feet there. And her flatmates seem very nice. A little strange, but very nice."

"I'm pleased I could help. This is my sister, Kathy. We're shopping for curtains."

"Pleased to meet you, Kathy." Dolly smiled a toothy grin.

"You too, Dolly," Kathy said. I could tell Kathy was desperate to ask who she was.

"I want to show my appreciation," Dolly said. "For helping Dorothy."

"There's really no need. You've done that already."

The 'portrait' she'd done of me was hidden away at the back of a cupboard in my flat.

"Perhaps I can do something for your sister?" She turned to Kathy. "Tell me dear, do you have a family?"

"I do. A husband, Peter, and we have two young children, Mikey and Lizzie."

"That's lovely. I'm an artist, you know. I'd love to paint a family portrait for you, if you'd allow me to?"

Oh no! I'd seen Dolly's paintings. They were rubbish.

"We'd love that," Kathy said, enthusiastically. "That's so very generous of you."

"My pleasure. Jill will give you my phone number. Give me a call to set up a date. Anyway, I must be getting back home. Bye, dears."

She began to walk away, but then suddenly stopped and turned back. "By the way, Jill — next time you're walking your dog, do call in and see Babs. She misses him so much."

When she'd gone, Kathy looked at me. "Dog? What dog?"

"I think she must have mixed me up with someone else."

Whoops!

Chapter 6

I hate the smell of paint.

I could smell it as soon as I walked into my office building. There were two workmen wearing white overalls: one at the top of a ladder, the other standing on the stairs. Zac Whiteside, my landlord, was just on his way out of the building.

"Hi Jill, how's it going?"

"Hi, Zac. I see you're sprucing the place up."

"Yeah. Your friend and mine, Gordon Armitage, has been on my back for some time now to decorate the common areas. Between you and me, I'm beginning to regret ever leasing the offices to him. He's more trouble than he's worth. He rings me up almost every week with some complaint or other. You, and your father before you, have had that office forever, and I don't think you've ever complained about anything."

"They're painting it orange?"

"That was Gordon's idea. Apparently orange is the corporate colour of Armitage, Armitage, Armitage and Poole. Although these are common areas, his company does occupy most of the building, so I agreed that we'd paint it in their colour. Anyway, I've got to go. See you around, Jill."

Paint was dripping from the brush held by the man on the ladder, onto the head of the smaller guy below him.

"Hey! Do you mind?" The smaller guy looked up; it was Blaze. Only then did I realise the person on the ladder was Daze.

"Sorry, Blaze," Daze said, but she didn't look very sorry.

"Hiya, Daze," I called.

"Hi, Jill. I thought this was where your office was."

"I take it this is your latest job—painting and decorating?"

"Yeah, I'm quite enjoying it. Although I'm not over fond of the orange."

"Me neither."

She came down the ladder, and joined Blaze and me on the stairs.

"What are you really doing here?" I said. "Are you on a case?"

"Yeah, we've had reports that a goblin has infiltrated the law firm that shares the building with you."

"What's he been up to?"

"Changing people's Wills."

"That's pretty despicable."

"Typical goblin," she said. "They're masters at it. They ingratiate themselves with people—usually the elderly, who are vulnerable, and then persuade them to change their Wills in favour of themselves. Anyway, we've marked this guy's card. We should have him out within a day or two."

"That's good, how's it going with Haze?"

"Okay, thanks. He's asked me to move in with him, but I haven't decided if I will or not yet. I need time to think about it; I don't want to rush into anything."

"What about you, Blaze, how's it going with Maze?"

"Okay, thanks. The only problem is she wants me to meet her parents, and between you and me, I'm a bit nervous about that."

"You'll be fine. I'd better get upstairs, and see what's waiting for me. See you both later."

***

When I walked into my office there was a large rectangular box—the size of a coffin—propped on two wooden stands on castors. What was going on now? This had Winky written all over it.

Then, he appeared, dressed in a dinner suit complete with bow tie.

"What are you up to, Winky?"

"What does it look like?"

"It looks like you're about to conduct a funeral."

That's when I noticed the digital recorder mounted on a tripod in the corner of the room.

"Are you recording this?"

"I will be doing in a minute."

"What exactly is it you're doing?" Did I really want to know?

"Recording my audition, obviously."

"How silly of me not to realise." I took a deep breath, and then let him have it. "What audition? And why is there a coffin in my office?"

He sighed. Winky had exasperation off to a fine art. "Firstly, this is not a coffin. It's a prop. Secondly, I'm taping my audition for The Meow Factor."

"Please tell me that isn't what I think it is."

"It's the biggest talent competition in the feline world."

"You mean like the X Factor?"

"Sort of. They copied the Meow Factor."

"Don't you have to go into the studios to audition?"

"No. Anyone can record and submit an audition of their act. The judges at Meow Factor view them all, and invite the top sixteen onto the live show."

"I'm really not sure the world is ready for an

undertaker/light entertainer."

"I'm not an undertaker. I'm The Great Winkini."

"The great what?"

"Winkini. The world's premier magician."

"Ah, right! That's why you're wearing that get-up. I still don't get the coffin, though."

"This prop is part of my act. Surely you've seen the 'saw the lady in half' trick?"

"Isn't that a little ambitious? Particularly if you're recording it? If anything goes wrong, the evidence is there for the police to see."

"Nothing will go wrong. You're talking to a professional here."

"Okay. Well, good luck with it. I don't envy whoever is going in the box."

He grinned.

"Hold on a minute. You surely don't think I—"

"Why not? All you have to do is lie down for a few minutes."

"If you think I'm getting into that box, and letting you come anywhere near me with a saw, you've got another think coming."

"Fair enough. I'll get Jules to do it."

"No, you can't involve that poor young girl."

"If you won't do it, what choice do I have?"

Poor old Jules. I was probably going to have to let her go. I could hardly put her through this ordeal too.

"Are you sure this is safe?"

"Of course. It's perfectly safe. This illusion has been performed thousands of times. "

"How many times have *you* performed it?"

"A few less than that."

"How many times?"

"I've watched the instruction video twice." He pushed a set of wooden steps in front of me. "Here, climb in."

"I'm not sure about this."

"I'll get Jules, then."

"Okay, okay."

I climbed up the steps, and into the box. As soon as I was inside, Winky closed the lid. There was a gap at the top where my head poked out.

"I'm having second thoughts about this."

Too late. I heard the click of the catches as he fastened them to stop me getting out.

"You will be careful, won't you?"

"Yeah. Don't worry. I've even put a plastic sheet on the floor in case there's any blood spatter."

"What?" I screamed.

"Only joking. I'll just go get the saw."

"I'm really not sure this is a good idea."

All of a sudden, I heard a buzzing sound.

"What's that?"

"Just the saw. Nothing to worry about."

"I thought you'd be using a handsaw."

"A chainsaw is much quicker."

"No! You can't—"

He began to cut through the box. I closed my eyes tight shut, and waited for the pain. Moments later, the buzzing stopped, and he spun me around. It was the weirdest sensation. I was looking at my feet which were sticking out from the other half of the box. I wiggled my toes just to be sure, and the toes in the other box wiggled.

I was freaked out, but also more than a little impressed.

"That was brilliant, Winky."

"The Great Winkini, please."

"Would you put me back together again now, please?"

"There's no point. The audition is finished."

"Winky! You can't leave me like this!"

"I suppose I could be persuaded."

"Salmon?"

"Red not pink, obviously."

"Obviously."

***

It was several days since the murder, and the library had now reopened. It was high time I had a look around there. The woman sitting behind the desk was wearing a badge which read: *'Acting Senior Librarian'*. Presumably, she'd had it made specially.

"Morning." She smiled. "Welcome to Washbridge library. Is there anything I can help you with today?"

"I'm not actually looking for a book. My name is Jill Gooder. I'm a private investigator. I'm investigating the murder of Anita Pick."

"Oh? Aren't the police dealing with that?"

"I'm working alongside them." Whether they like it or not. "Did you know Anita well?"

She glanced left and right, as though she wanted to make sure no one could overhear.

"Quite well. Or, at least as well as anyone *could* get to know that woman. To be honest, I always found her a little cold—and she could be really spiteful sometimes."

"Spiteful, how?"

"I applied for a Senior Librarian position at another library; I'd rather not name it. But when I asked her if she'd support my application, she refused. She said I didn't have the necessary experience, which is total rubbish. I've been doing the job for over eight years; I know just as much about the library as Anita."

"I see. Can you think of any reason why someone would want to murder her?"

"No, certainly not. She wasn't my favourite person, but I have no idea why anyone would want to do her harm."

"Have you worked in this particular library recently?"

"On and off. I tend to move around between several libraries—filling in as necessary to cover absence and holidays."

"Is it okay if I take a look around?"

"Yes, of course. Help yourself."

The library was old and in need of some renovation. Apart from a lot of books, there really wasn't much else to see. There didn't appear to be any security cameras inside the building, so on my way out I checked with the Acting Senior Librarian.

"I can't see any CCTV cameras inside the building. Is that right?"

"There isn't the money for them, and anyway, what would people steal? A few books? It wouldn't be worth it these days. There are cameras outside which cover the main doors."

"I didn't notice them when I came in."

"They're actually obscured a little by the tree."

"But they still work, do they?"

"I don't actually know, but I assume so."

"Would it be possible to see the recordings?"

"That's all dealt with by an external security company. I believe the same company covers all the libraries in the region. I can find you the name if you like. You could leave me your number, and I'll call you with the details."

"Thanks. That would be very helpful."

***

Aunt Lucy had sent a message that she wanted to see me, so I magicked myself over to her house.

"Thanks for coming, Jill. Would you like a cup of tea and a custard cream? I got some in specially for you."

"Go on then, if you're twisting my arm."

She made tea, and we settled down in the kitchen with a plate of custard creams in front of us. There were six on the plate. So that was four for me and two for Aunt Lucy. What? I'm only joking. Sheesh.

"What did you want to talk to me about, Aunt Lucy?"

"A friend of mine, Coral Fish, is the curator of the Candlefield Museum of Witchcraft."

"I didn't know there was such a place."

"It's on the other side of Candlefield, so you probably won't have seen it. Anyway, it seems their most important exhibit has been stolen: The Wand of Magna."

"Wand? I didn't think witches used wands?"

"They never have really, but a long time ago they used to carry them as a sort of symbol; a representation of their magical powers. It was a silly tradition, but it was one that no one seemed to dare challenge. Until Magna Mondale."

"She's the one the wand is named after?"

"That's right, it's actually her wand. Magna emerged as the most powerful witch of her time, and probably of all time. Up until that point, there'd only ever been five levels. But she was so much more powerful than any other witch, that level six was created just for her."

"Why haven't I heard about her before?"

"If you'd been brought up in Candlefield, and had attended school here, you would have. It's taught as part of the history of witchcraft. Even so, because it's so long ago now it's not something that many young people can relate to. One of the first things Magna did when she became the first level six witch, was to discard her wand. And, she encouraged all other witches to do the same. A few didn't like the idea, and resisted. But over time, the wand was consigned to history."

"I see. So this wand—the one that's gone missing—it doesn't actually have any magical powers?"

"No. None of them ever did. It's purely a symbol. But it's also a record of one of the most important stages in the history of Candlefield witches."

"Have the police been informed?"

"No. Coral doesn't want news of the theft to spread. She's afraid that if the police are notified, the press will find out soon after, and then it will be all over Candlefield."

"But won't people notice it's missing?"

"No, because they have a duplicate, which they use whenever the actual wand has to be taken away for cleaning. So, for the time being, they've put that in its place. But it's only going to be a matter of time before someone realises."

Chapter 7

It was no good. I couldn't justify keeping Jules on as my PA. The only experience she had was in packing sausages and black puddings. Times were hard, and I could barely make rent, so how could I pay her to sit at a desk looking pretty? It's not as though she could even use a computer. Sometimes you have to be cruel to be kind. I'd just have to tell her the truth — well, not the entire truth. I could hardly tell her that my cat had recruited her. I'd just say that setting her on had been a mistake, and I'd have to let her go.

I felt bad about it, but with her experience in the food packing industry, I felt sure she'd get another job soon — maybe packing pickles? Winky wouldn't be very pleased with me, but this was all his fault anyway.

Even though I knew it was the right thing to do, I wasn't looking forward to telling her. Poor little mite. She'd been so pleased to be starting a new career as a PA, and now I was going to burst her bubble.

I gave myself a silent pep talk as I walked up the stairs to my offices.

"Come on Jill, you've got to be strong! You're a business woman. You can't let sentiment rule your head."

I was going to do it first thing. There was no point in delaying. Jules would be upset and she might even cry, but it had to be done. I took a deep breath and walked in.

"Morning, Jill!" She greeted me with a cheery smile.

Oh bum! This wasn't going to be easy.

"Morning, Jules." She looked so happy. "There's something I need to—"

"Jill, look, before you say anything, there's something I have to tell you."

"What's that?"

"I have to resign, I'm afraid."

Do what?

"Oh dear, and you were doing so well. Is the job too much for you? Are you going back to the black pudding factory?"

"No, I would never go back there. I've actually had a better offer."

"A better offer? Doing what?"

"To work as a receptionist."

"But you've only been here a few days."

"I know! Brilliant, isn't it? I always thought that once I had my foot on the ladder, I'd have more opportunities, but I never dreamed it would happen so quickly."

"That's great, I guess. Do you mind me asking where you're going to work?"

"That's the other good thing. It's not very far away. In fact, it's right next door—for those lawyer people."

"You mean Armitage, Armitage, Armitage and Poole?

"Yes. That's them. There's a lot of Armitages, aren't there? In fact, it was one of the Armitages who came in to see me just fifteen minutes ago."

"Was it Gordon Armitage, by any chance?"

"Yes. I think that was his name. He said he'd spotted me, and thought I'd make the ideal receptionist for his company. He offered me a job there and then. It's a lot more money than you were going to pay me, so I had to accept. I'm sorry to let you down, but I could hardly say no."

"Of course not. I'm sorry to lose you, obviously."

What? Who are you calling a hypocrite?

"Is it okay if I go around there now? He said I could start today."

"Yes, of course."

I left Jules packing her stuff, and went through to my office. I didn't know how to feel about what had just happened. I'd wanted her gone, but for Armitage to come in here and poach my staff was simply malicious. He must have realised that Jules wasn't a qualified receptionist; he'd done it just to get at me.

"What's the matter with Jules?" Winky said.

"She's leaving."

"How could you fire her? Have you no heart?"

"Hold on. I haven't fired anyone. I like Jules. I was quite happy for her to stay."

"So why is she leaving then?"

"It's that crowd next door: Armitage, Armitage, Armitage and Poole. They've offered her a job with more money."

"See? Can I spot talent or what? Do you want me to find a replacement for her?"

"Don't you dare!"

***

Anita Pick's husband, Gregory, lived in one of the more affluent parts of Washbridge. I knew as soon as I saw the address that we were talking about a property worth several million pounds.

I couldn't even see the house because it was hidden away behind a high wall. The gate was locked, so I pressed the button on the intercom.

"Hello." A stern voice came back.

"Hello there. I'm hoping to see Gregory Pick."

"Do you have an appointment?"

"No. My name is Jill Gooder—I'm a private investigator. I'm investigating the murder of Mr Pick's wife."

"Just a moment." The intercom clicked off. I wasn't optimistic about being allowed in, so I began to consider the various spells which I might use to gain access. But then, the same voice came back through the intercom. "Come up to the house, please."

I drove slowly up the driveway. The gardens were magnificent, as was the huge fountain.

Before I could ring the doorbell, a butler opened the door, and invited me inside.

"Please follow me, madam. Mr Pick is in the main reception room."

The house reeked of money—from the marble floor to the chandeliers. The numerous paintings were no doubt collector's items.

Gregory Pick greeted me with a smile, which was anything but genuine. "I understand that you're investigating Anita's murder. Who hired you, if you don't mind me asking?"

"My friend, Madeline Lane. She's been charged with your wife's murder."

"She must be the Assistant Librarian?"

"That's right."

"I take it you don't think she's responsible?"

"I know she isn't. Madeline could never do anything like that."

"I see. And how can I help, exactly?"

"When was the last time you saw Anita?"

"A week before she was murdered, but only briefly, at my

solicitor's office. You do know that we were going through divorce proceedings, I assume?"

"Yes, I'm aware of that."

"As always, she was being awkward—very awkward indeed. I've done my best to reach a fair settlement which would allow both of us to move on with our lives."

"Pickle!" The voice came from my right. I turned around to see a tall, slim, attractive, young woman. She was six feet two if she was an inch. "Pickle, have you seen Boo-Boo?"

"Lily Bell, come over here, darling. There's someone I'd like you to meet."

She walked over to us as though she was on a catwalk.

"Lily Bell. This is—sorry I've forgotten your name."

"Jill Gooder."

"Of course. This is Jill Gooder. She's a private investigator; she's looking into Anita's murder."

At the mention of Anita's name, Lily Bell's smile turned into a scowl. "Why does she need to speak to you?"

"She's just asking a few questions, darling."

"That woman has been the bane of our lives. I can't say I'm sorry she's gone."

"Lily Bell—darling—you mustn't say things like that."

"It's true though. Isn't it, Pickle? She was trying to squeeze every last penny out of you."

"Is that true?" I asked Pick.

"Of course it is," Lily Bell answered for him. "And why should she have all of his money? It's not like she ever supported him. If anything, she held him back."

"I think you'd better go and look for Boo-Boo." Pick seemed a little embarrassed by Lily Bell's outburst.

"Okay, Pickle. Love you lots." She left with the same

catwalk elegance.

"Boo-Boo?" I said.

"Lily Bell's poodle."

The contrast between Anita, who I'd met briefly on two occasions, and Lily Bell was unbelievable.

"Can I ask how you and Anita met?"

"At Uni. Anita was reading English Lit. I was studying I.T. — Artificial Intelligence mainly."

"You've obviously done well for yourself."

"Yes, I struck lucky during the dot com boom, and then I sold up. Now I spend most of my time playing golf and tennis." He laughed. "It's a tough job, but someone has to do it."

"I assume Anita stood to benefit substantially from the divorce?"

"The woman was asking for half of everything. Why should she get half just for being married to me? It's not like she played any part in the business, whatsoever — if anything she held me back." He seemed to realise the implications of what he'd said. "Of course, that doesn't mean I wished her ill. I was devastated to hear about her death."

"Can you think of anyone who would have wanted to kill Anita?"

"No one. Surely, this is just a random killing, isn't it? The library has always attracted more than its fair share of nutjobs."

"You may be right."

It was certainly a strong possibility.

After we were done, Pick showed me to the door.

"I hope you find who did this. Anita was a pain in the backside, but she didn't deserve to die like that."

He sounded sincere, but then they always did.

***

Kathy had phoned to tell me that Dolly was on her way over to paint their family portrait. I had to stop this travesty somehow, so I jumped in the car, and hurried over there.

"Kathy, I really don't think this is a good idea."

"What's your problem? Pete and I like the idea of a family portrait."

She and Peter had changed into their Sunday best clothes.

"Why do I have to wear this?" Mikey said, pulling at his bow tie. He and Lizzie were dressed up too.

"Leave your bow tie alone." Kathy straightened it again. "A lady is coming to paint our portrait."

"Can I have my drum in the picture?"

"No," Kathy snapped. "I don't want that thing in the painting."

"Do I look nice, Auntie Jill?" Lizzie said.

"Yes, Lizzie. You look like a little angel."

"Mummy says I can't have any of my beanies in the picture."

"Probably for the best." I turned to Kathy. "Can I have a word?" I ushered her into the kitchen. "Look. I don't know how to say this, but—err—Dolly—err—she isn't really a —"

I was interrupted by a knock on the door.

"That must be her!" Kathy rushed to answer it. I followed.

"Come in, Dolly," Kathy gushed. "Do you need a hand with your equipment? Pete, come and help Dolly to carry her things in. Where do you want us?"

Dolly followed Kathy into the living room. "Probably over by that wall. That would make a nice backdrop."

"How long will this take, Mum?" Mikey said. "I want to practise my drum."

Dolly smiled at him. "It won't take very long, young man."

Oh well, no one could say I hadn't tried.

"I think I'll be off."

"Why don't you stay and watch, Jill?" Peter said.

"No, it's okay. I'd better get going."

I didn't want to hang around to witness the fallout.

***

Two hours later, I was back at my flat when my phone rang; it was Kathy. Oh no! I knew what this was about, and I really didn't want to have to deal with it.

 "Why didn't you warn me?" Kathy shouted.

"About what?"

"You know what! Dolly! She can't draw for toffee."

"I did try to tell you."

"It was so embarrassing. We all look like matchstick men."

"Lowry did all right with them."

"Lowry this is not! Even Mikey said it was rubbish."

"He didn't say that out loud did he?"

"Yes, but I don't think Dolly heard him. I told him to go and play with his drum."

"I did try to warn you."

"But she called herself an artist."

"I know. I think she truly believes that's what she is."

"How do you know her anyway?"

"I helped her daughter to get a job in that fancy dress shop we went to, and also to find a flat-share."

"Where does Dolly live?"

"Out of town somewhere. I'm not sure where."

"Something funny is going on here. What was all that about a dog?"

"I have no idea. You've seen her paintings. She's a lovely old dear, but she's definitely a cucumber short of a sandwich."

"Isn't that supposed to be a sandwich short of a picnic?"

"Whatever. The scary thing is that she normally charges for her work."

Chapter 8

I had a meeting with Anita Pick's solicitor, a man named Larry Long, who had been acting for her in the divorce. His was a small practice, which comprised of just him and one other partner, a Mr Stephen Short. They were based in a building that was only two doors down from my own.

"Good morning, Madam." The young female receptionist greeted me with a dazzling smile. I wondered if she had a background in black pudding packing too. "Do you have an appointment?"

"Mr Long is expecting me. My name is Jill Gooder."

"Please take a seat. Mr Long will be with you shortly."

Long? Shortly? While I waited, I contemplated the comedy gold opportunities presented by their names.

"Miss Gooder?" A man appeared from one of the two offices to my left. He was tiny.

"Call me Jill, please."

"I'm Larry Long. Pleased to meet you."

We shook hands, and then I followed him into his office.

"How can I help you, Jill?"

"I was hoping to get some information about Anita Pick's divorce."

"Terrible business. I couldn't believe it when I heard the news. There's a limit to what I can tell you, obviously, for confidentiality reasons. What I can say though, is the poor woman was being put through the mill. Have you met her husband?"

"Yes, I went to his house the other day. He seemed perfectly pleasant."

"Don't be fooled. He can be charming, but he's totally ruthless when it comes to money. Have you met his new love interest? Lily something—"

"Lily Bell?"

"That's the one. She's got her claws into him in a big way, and even though Pick is ruthless, we could have probably reached a settlement if it wasn't for that woman. Lily Bell is adamant that he should fight for every last penny. As a result, he's been trying to squirrel away cash and other assets to reduce the settlement. But it hasn't done him much good because we've uncovered most of it. Anita stood to make a pretty penny."

"What will happen now?"

"As no settlement has been reached, and they aren't yet divorced, it will depend on what's in her Will—always assuming there is one. They have no children, so my guess is that Pick will end up with the lot."

After we'd finished, Larry walked me back through reception. As he did, a giant of a man appeared out of the adjacent office.

"Jill, can I introduce you to my partner, Stephen Short."

***

I was on my way to Candlefield Museum. I'd never been to that part of Candlefield before; it was more than a little off the beaten track.

Coral Fish was about the same age as Aunt Lucy. But that's where the resemblance ended. Whereas Aunt Lucy was very colourful and a teeny bit eccentric, Coral was dressed all in grey, and came across as being very strait-laced.

She led me into her office. "Thank you for agreeing to help, Jill."

"My pleasure."

"Has your Aunt Lucy told you about the wand?"

"Yes, she gave me some background. I have to confess I hadn't even heard of it until then. In fact, I didn't know this museum existed until she told me about it."

"We are a bit out of the way here, but there's a reason for that. It's built on the site of Magna Mondale's house."

"Who knows the wand is missing?"

"Myself, Bert Hee, the night security man, Elizabeth Myles, the art restorer, and Sandra Bell, head of P.R. and marketing. Bert discovered it was missing quite early in the morning. I was holding a meeting in my office at the time with Julie and Sandra. Bert came bursting in, and blurted out what had happened. I trust them all to be discreet, so I don't think news of this will leak from within these walls."

"I'm going to need your permission to talk to those three members of staff."

"Yes, of course. I'm sure they'll be only too pleased to help."

"And, I'll need permission to explore all areas of the museum."

"No problem. Except for the sealed room, of course."

"Sealed room?"

"As I mentioned earlier, this museum was built on the site of Magna Mondale's house. Over her lifetime, she developed many new and powerful spells, but she feared they might be used for evil, so she sealed them away to prevent that from happening. The original house was demolished to make way for this museum, which over the years has been extended. But the sealed room in the basement remains untouched from when it formed part of

Magna's house."

"Has anyone ever been in that room?"

"Several people have tried, but no one has been able to overcome the spell which Magna herself cast to seal it."

"Can I see it?"

"You can see the door to the room. You'll find it in the basement."

"Do you have any theories as to why the wand has been taken?"

"Nothing concrete. I suppose it's possible someone may have done it for financial gain."

"Does it have a monetary value?"

"Not on the open market. Anyone trying to sell it would be reported immediately. But on the black market, who knows? There are collectors who might jump at the chance of owning it."

"Do you know of any?"

"Not by name, but I know they exist."

"Okay, thanks. If it's alright with you, I'll take a look around now."

I hadn't gone far when I bumped into Bert Hee; an elderly wizard with greying hair who stooped a little when he walked.

"Hello, young lady. I understand you're here to find our wand."

"I'm going to do my best, Mr Hee."

"Call me Bert—everyone does."

"Okay, Bert. I'm Jill."

"I know all about you. You're Mirabel's granddaughter, aren't you?"

"That's right. Do you know her?"

"Oh yes. When she was young, she was quite the wild child."

"Really? Tell me more."

"Not likely." He grinned. "Your grandmother would hunt me down, and do unspeakable things to me."

He was probably right. Pity, I would have loved to have heard more about Grandma and her misspent youth.

"Can I ask you a few questions, Bert?"

"Of course, dear. I'll be only too pleased to help if I can."

"How long have you been doing this job?"

"Almost thirty years now."

"Have there been many similar incidents during that time?"

"Not a single break-in all the time I've been here. But then there's nothing of any real value in here. Lots of items have a 'cultural' value, but they're not the sort of thing to attract the criminal element."

"Did you hear or see anything unusual the night the wand went missing?"

"Nothing at all. It was just like any other night—just me and the shadows." He hesitated. "There is one thing I probably ought to mention, though."

"What's that?"

"It's a bit of a confession, actually. If I tell you, will you promise not to tell Coral?"

"Of course."

"The truth is, I fell asleep. It's the first time I've ever done it in the thirty years I've worked here. It must have been around four a.m. I didn't wake up until nine-thirty; I should have finished at seven o'clock. That's when I discovered the wand was missing. You won't tell Coral I fell asleep, will you?"

"No, I promise. Your secret is safe with me."

***

On my way home, I dropped into the newsagent across the road from my flat, to pick up a bottle of ginger beer. Jasper James was behind the counter, wearing a purple fedora with the letters JJ on the front.

"Hello, Jill," he said. "Did you decide to subscribe to P.I. Monthly?"

"I'm not going to bother, thanks. I did read it, but there wasn't really anything new in it. It was all recycled stuff that I already know. I'll just take the ginger beer, please."

"I might have a magazine that you *would* be interested in."

"I doubt it. I'm not really a big reader. I don't have the time."

"I think you'll want to see this one." He came from behind the counter, walked down the display of magazines, picked one out, and held it up for me to see.

"Custard Cream Quarterly? Wow! Yes, I'm definitely interested in that."

"I thought you would be. Would you like me to put one aside for you once a quarter?"

"Yes, please. How much is it?"

"Eight pounds fifty."

"How much?" I gasped.

"It's rather a niche magazine."

"I suppose so. Still, worth every penny."

When I left, I spotted Mr Ivers walking across the road. He was obviously on his way to the newsagent, too.

"Hi there, Mr Ivers."

"Hello." He was stony-faced. His eyes looked glazed.

"Are you okay, Mr Ivers?"

"Yes, thank you."

"Are you sure?"

"Yes, thank you."

"Have you seen any good movies this week?"

"No."

"Right. Have you seen Tess recently?"

"Yes. Goodbye." With that, he carried on walking.

Something wasn't right. In fact, something was very wrong indeed. He looked like he'd been drugged.

This had to be Alicia's doing.

Back in my flat, I couldn't settle. I was concerned about Mr Ivers. He'd looked like a zombie, and I was worried that Alicia may have done to him what she'd once done to me. I needed help, and the only person I could turn to was Grandma. My magazine would just have to wait.

I drove back into town, and made my way to Ever A Wool Moment. Grandma was in the back office.

"Ah, Jill. I'm glad you called in. I wanted to let you know that The Candle intend to run an article on the Compass competition. You, me and the other team members will need to get together for a team photograph."

"Okay, Grandma. But look—the reason I came to see you is that I'm rather worried about one of my neighbours, Mr Ivers."

"Is he bothering you? Would you like me to turn him into a cockroach?"

"No."

"A slug?"

"No, no, nothing like that. I think he might have been poisoned, and I think Alicia did it. She's been posing as

Tess again. He met her through the Love Spell dating agency. I've got a feeling she's done to him what she did to me before the Elite competition. He's really not himself, and he doesn't look at all well."

"Why are you telling me all this?"

"I want you to help him."

"Why? He's only a human."

"What do you mean, *only* a human? Humans are every bit as important as sups."

"Don't be ridiculous."

"My adoptive family are humans."

"So?"

"Please, Grandma, I need you to help him like you helped me when I'd been poisoned."

"What's in it for me?"

"If you do this, I'll owe you a favour."

"I like the sound of that." Her face lit up. "Come to think of it, my bunions have been playing up recently."

Oh bum!

"So, will you help him?"

"I suppose so, as long as it doesn't take too long."

"We have to do it now — before it's too late."

"You'd better magic us over there, then."

"Me? Magic both of us over there?"

"I don't know where he lives, do I? Here — take my hand." Her bony fingers always gave me the creeps.

I cast the spell, and the next moment, the two of us were inside Mr Ivers' flat. He was lying on the sofa, and looked totally zonked out. I waved my hand in front of his face, but there was no reaction at all.

"He's a very plain-looking man, isn't he?" Grandma said.

"Grandma — focus! Has he been poisoned?"

"Oh, yes. He's definitely been poisoned. He's under Alicia's control. She'll probably kill him when she's had enough of him. Right, I'd better be getting back."

"Hold on. We can't leave him like this!"

"I thought you just wanted me to tell you what was the matter with him."

"No, I want you to do something about it."

"Very well. You'd better go and get me a cup of water."

I went through to the kitchen, found a cup and filled it with cold water.

"There you go."

She put it on the coffee table, and proceeded to take all manner of ingredients from somewhere inside her cardigan. Whatever they were, they smelled revolting. After she'd sprinkled them into the cup, she stirred the mixture.

"That should do it. Get him to drink all of that. He'll be as right as rain within thirty minutes or so."

"What about when Alicia comes back? Won't she just do it to him again?"

"How very tiresome." Grandma waved a hand, and I could tell that she'd cast a spell of some kind. "He'll be okay now."

"What was that spell you cast?"

"It's the 'wicked witch away' spell. No wicked witch will be able to come within three metres of him from now on, so he'll be perfectly safe."

"What about me? Am I all right to stay here?"

"Are you wicked? Is there something you're not telling me, Jill?"

"No, no, of course not."

"Then you'll be fine."

Chapter 9

Winky was glued to the window. No, not literally — just how cruel do you think I am?

"Are you looking for Bella?"

"No. She's at the cat grooming parlour today."

"What's so interesting out there, then? I hope you aren't flirting with another cat."

"If you must know, my brother is coming to stay."

"When you say 'stay'? Do you mean 'visit'?"

"In case you haven't already noticed, I have an extensive vocabulary. If I'd meant 'visit', I would have said 'visit'. I meant he's coming to stay."

"What about me?"

"It's okay — he won't mind you being here. He's used to witches."

"I meant what about *asking* me if it's okay? I might not want another cat in the office. Particularly if he's as much trouble as you."

"*I'm* no trouble. Anyway, Socks is nothing like me."

"Socks? Is he called that because he has white paws?"

"No, it's because he used to smell like old socks."

"Great."

"It's okay. He's grown out of it."

"When is he coming?"

"Anytime now."

"Is his owner bringing him over?"

"When are you going to get it, Jill? Cats don't have *owners*. He'll be arriving by microlight. Which reminds me — I'd better open this window."

"Hold on! Are you trying to tell me that he's going to land a microlight in this office?"

"That's right. Socks is an expert when it comes to the microlight."

The window was still open an hour later, but there was no sign of Winky's aerobatic brother.

"Can we shut this window? I'm freezing."

"No. Socks will be here any minute now."

"I'm still not sure this is a good idea. It sounds really dangerous to me. Couldn't he land somewhere close by — maybe in a field — and just walk from there?"

"You worry too much. My bro knows what he's doing."

"Your *bro*?"

Just then, I heard the sound of a small motor.

"It's Socks. Look! He's over there." Winky pointed over the roof tops of the buildings opposite.

"Does he have a pilot's license for that thing?"

"Of course he does. He's not irresponsible."

"What's he doing now? Why did he suddenly plummet down like that?"

"It must be the down-draught between the buildings."

"Is he okay?"

Winky looked a little worried. "I hope so."

We both watched as Socks tried to combat the strong downward gusts.

"He's not going to make it," I yelled.

"Yes, he will. He'll be okay."

"I don't think —"

"Look out!"

We both dived for cover as the microlight came sailing in through the window, and slid to a halt at the far side of the room. Winky dashed over to his brother.

"Socks! Socks, are you okay?"

The black and white cat climbed out of the microlight, discarded his helmet and goggles, and embraced his brother. "Good to see you again, bro."

***

I drove over to Anita Pick's house. I wanted to speak to her neighbour—a woman called Roxy Blackwall. Mad had told me that Anita and her neighbour had been involved in some sort of long-running dispute.

As soon as I arrived at Anita's house, I could see the source of the friction. In the back garden of the neighbouring house were at least seven, maybe eight, dogs running loose. There was a mix of sizes and breeds, and they all began to bark as soon as they heard me. I wasn't in any danger because they couldn't get over the fence, but it was still quite intimidating. I could see how this situation might have upset Anita.

As I looked over at the dogs, the door to the neighbouring house opened, and a woman stepped out. She was short with greying hair—perhaps in her early fifties. She was wearing some kind of uniform—an ambulance driver or paramedic.

"Can I help you?" she said.

"Are you Roxy Blackwall?"

"Who wants to know?"

"My name is Jill Gooder. I'm a private investigator. I'm looking into Anita's murder."

"I couldn't believe it when I heard the news." She shook her head. "Although I have to be honest, she and I never really did get on."

"What was the reason for that, if you don't mind me

asking?"

"She was always complaining about my dogs."

"You do have rather a lot of them."

"Yes, but they're all very well behaved."

"What in particular did she complain about?"

"Oh, everything. It's a pity she didn't have anything better to worry about. If she'd seen the sights I see on a daily basis, then maybe she wouldn't have worried about a few dogs barking. I see plenty of human tragedy day in, day out, and I can tell you there are more important things in life to worry about than a few dogs."

"I understand from the Assistant Librarian that you went into the library, and had words with Anita not too long ago."

"That's right, and with good cause. I could put up with Anita's constant complaining, but then she went and poisoned Jo Jo."

"Jo Jo?"

"She was my setter. Anita killed her."

"Do you have any proof of that?"

"No, of course not. I went to the police, but they didn't want to know. But I know it was her. That's why I went to the library—I would have throttled her if her assistant hadn't pulled me off. It's probably just as well she did, or I'd have been doing time, and who would have looked after these then?"

The dogs were getting louder, and seemed to be even more excitable.

"You'll have to excuse me. It's their dinner time."

"Okay. Thanks for your help."

***

I ran over the Anita Pick case in my mind. It seemed to me there were several people who had a motive for killing her.

The most obvious candidate was Anita's husband, Gregory Pick. He'd stood to lose half of his money to Anita in the divorce settlement. Now she was dead, he'd probably get to keep the lot. And of course, there was his new woman, Lily Bell. She seemed even more keen to hang on to the money than Gregory.

Then there was June Fleming, the Acting Senior Librarian. She obviously felt aggrieved that Anita Pick had refused to recommend her for the Senior Librarian vacancy. But, was that a good enough reason to kill someone? It shouldn't have been, but people have murdered for far less.

Roxy Blackwall hadn't liked Anita Pick, and maybe with good reason if Anita had poisoned her dog.

Or of course, it could have been a random stranger. To my mind, that was still a very strong possibility.

***

As soon as I got back to my office building, I could hear voices on the landing. It was Gordon Armitage; he was with another man who was older and a little shorter. Unsurprisingly, Armitage seemed to be doing most of the talking. The other man got in the occasional, *'But Gordon, I really think'*, and *'I'm not so sure that's a good idea, Gordon'*. But Armitage spoke over him every time. What a rude and obnoxious man Gordon Armitage was.

When I was about halfway up the stairs, Armitage noticed

me, and immediately stopped talking to the shorter man.

"Well." He glared at me. "If it isn't our resident squatter, Miss Gooder."

I took a deep breath. I had to resist the urge to turn him into a toad.

"I seem to recall, Gordon, that I was here first."

The other man looked distinctly uncomfortable about our exchange.

"Maybe. But it's only a matter of time before you move out. From what I hear, you're barely making enough money to keep the lights on. I understand your receptionist quit earlier today."

"Only because you poached her."

"She'll have a bright future with Armitage, Armitage, Armitage and Poole—which is more than you could ever offer her."

Little did he know that he'd done me a favour taking Jules off my hands.

"Move out of my way, Gordon or I'll be forced to knock out *your* lights."

"Threats? Not very professional, Miss Gooder." He stepped aside.

Once in the office, I was about to slam the door closed behind me when I realised the little man had followed me.

"Did you want something?"

"Sorry. No—err—I was just looking for—never mind, sorry." And with that, he disappeared.

Who *was* that funny little man? One of Armitage's minions, I assumed.

***

My big mouth had landed me with the job of putting together a women's team for the charity BoundBall match. Instead of shelling out for an expensive advert, I'd contacted the sports desk at The Candle and told them what I was planning. They seemed keen to cover the story, and said they'd send a reporter out to talk to me.

I didn't want to do the interview in Cuppy C; it was a little too public. So instead, I'd asked Aunt Lucy if I could meet with the reporter at her house, and she'd readily agreed.

He was due to arrive any minute.

"Well, Jill, you've really surpassed yourself this time." Grandma had decided to show her face.

"What do you mean?"

"This crazy idea of yours—women versus men at BoundBall. Are you insane?"

"I thought you of all people, would be supportive. Surely you don't buy into the *men are better than women* argument."

"Of course not. Men are far inferior, but women have never played BoundBall, so of course they're not going to win."

"I fully intend that our team *will* win."

"If you must go through with this charade, please keep my name out of the paper. I may want to run for the Town Council again next year. Being associated with this debacle won't do me any good at all."

"In that case, Grandma, I suggest you leave now because the reporter from The Candle will be here any minute."

"Oh? I'd better be going then."

Good riddance!

"Look, Jill, you can still back out of this, you know," Aunt

Lucy said. "I'm sure Annie Christy would understand. There are plenty of other things you could do to raise funds."

"It's too late now. I've already told The Candle."

There was a knock at the door.

"It sounds like he's here." Aunt Lucy stood up. "I'll go and let him in, and then leave you to it."

"Jill Gooder I assume?" the ruddy faced man said.

"Yeah, that's me."

"I'm Don Roming from The Candle sports desk. I assume all this BoundBall business is a joke, is it?"

"Why would you think that?"

"You can't seriously be planning to take on a men's team, can you?"

"That's exactly what we're planning to do. It's for charity — for SupAid."

"I believe the men are giving you a start?"

"Yes, a hundred points."

"Is that all? You'd need a thousand, and even then you'd struggle."

"Look, I hope you're going to do a balanced article."

"Of course, what else?"

Throughout the interview, he was both condescending and patronising, but I managed to keep my cool because I needed his help. When he'd finished asking questions, I said, "Look, there's just one more thing."

"What's that, dear?"

"I'd like you to include an appeal for women interested in joining our team to get in touch with me."

He laughed. "Does that mean you don't actually have a team yet?"

"Not a full team, no."

"How many players do you have?"

"Not enough to make a team, as yet. So, will you include the appeal?"

"Of course. For what good it will do."

After he'd gone, I was seething. The man was a complete moron. Well, we'd show him, and all the other men who doubted us.

Chapter 10

The next morning, as I walked up the stairs, I could hear sounds coming from the outer office. Had Winky recruited another receptionist? Perhaps someone from the fish packing industry this time?

"Mrs V? You're back!"

"Hello, Jill."

"How are things with your sister?"

"When I got down there, G was sitting up in a hospital bed, looking as fit as I'd ever seen her."

"But I thought you said it was her heart?"

"It was just exhaustion. It seems she'd been doing another marathon knitting session, and she'd obviously overdone it. The fatigue must have got to her, but they ran an ECG and did blood tests. She's perfectly fine."

"So she didn't mind you coming back?"

"Oh, she minded all right. She said if I cared about her, I'd stay down there for a few weeks and help her with the housework and the shopping, and anything else she could dream up. I told her, if she thinks I'm going to be her slave, she's got another think coming!"

"It's so good to have you back, Mrs V."

"It's good to *be* back. Did you have to get someone in?"

"Well, yes and no. We had a young girl called Jules, but she wasn't here for very long. She was poached by that lot next door."

"Armitage?"

"Yes. Actually, they did me a favour. She wasn't really qualified to be a receptionist. She'd only had experience in the sausage and black pudding packing industries."

"How very unusual. How did she get the job in the first

place?"

"It's a long story. Maybe some other time. Anyway, would you like a cup of tea?"

"That would be lovely, dear. I'll unpack my knitting and crocheting, and get back to work."

***

I'd spoken briefly to Jack about Anita Pick's murder. As always, he'd played his cards close to his chest.

"What about Roxy Blackwall? She told me that she'd reported her dog had been poisoned, but the police did nothing about it."

"That's not true. I checked back on our records. There was a spate of dog poisonings at the time — all setters. We caught the guy not long after Roxy Blackwall's dog was killed."

"She still seems to be under the impression it was Anita Pick who did it."

"One of our uniformed officers should have updated her. And besides, it was all over The Bugle."

"Washbridge's quality tabloid?"

"None other."

I'd asked Jack if he'd have a word with the security company, so they'd allow me to view their CCTV. He hadn't been very enthusiastic at first, but then I reminded him that I'd spotted something his people had missed during the 'murder in the lift' case, and he eventually agreed to let me take a look at it.

The security company confirmed what June Fleming had already told me, that the only security cameras active around the library were those focused on the front door.

Jack had said I should ask for a Mr Saize.

"Jill?" A young man with spiky black hair came bouncing into reception.

"Mr Saize?"

"Please call me Simon."

Simon Saize? Priceless!

"What exactly are you looking for?" Simon said.

"I don't actually know. Can I just go through the tape for that day? Is that possible?"

"Certainly — Detective Maxwell said we were to give you full access." Simon led me to a small office which had a single desk and a chair. Then he logged into the computer, set up the recording, and walked me through the controls. "If you need anything, just pick up that phone, and dial two-three-five."

I was working a hunch. I knew Mad hadn't murdered Anita, so there had to be at least one other person in the library after the doors had been locked. My plan was to count everyone who entered or left the library from the moment the doors opened in the morning until they were locked again in the evening. It was going to be a long, boring job, which was why I'd brought a packet of custard creams and a can of ginger beer with me.

I started the recording from the point where the doors were due to be opened. There were already four people waiting outside. I had a notepad, and for every person who went in, I made a stroke on the top of the page, and for every person who left the building, I made a stroke at the bottom of the page. Even though I was fast-forwarding through the tape, it was still a soul-destroying task, but I could think of no other way to do it. The only other way into the building was through the fire escapes. But, if someone had used those, they would have set off the alarm, and there had been no reports of it going off on that day.

Another two people in—three out. The time on the recording showed it was mid-afternoon. Two more in—four out. At long last, I could see that the doors had been locked. My figures showed two hundred and twenty people in; two hundred and nineteen people out. That meant one person was still in the building, unless I'd missed someone or wrongly recorded the numbers. I was now fairly confident that someone else was still in the building after the library had shut.

A few minutes later, Simon came in to check on me.

"How's it going?"

"Okay, thanks, but the next part is going to take much longer."

"What exactly are you looking for?"

I explained my theory—that someone was still in the building when the doors were locked.

"Now, I need to find out *who* it was. The only way to do that is to go through the tape again, and make a brief note about each person who enters the building—a simple description should suffice. Then, as each person leaves the building, I can cross that person from my list. If my theory works, I should be able to identify the person who didn't leave."

"I could do that for you, if you like?"

"You?"

"For a small fee."

"How small?"

"A hundred pounds?"

It was hardly a 'small' fee, but it was well worth it if it saved me from having to do it.

"When?"

"I'll have to do it in between working my own job, so it might take a few days, but I could start straight away if you like?"

"That would be great."

"I'll need fifty pounds up front."

"I'll give you thirty now, and the rest when you've identified the person who went into the building, but didn't come out."

"Done."

***

Winky was fast asleep on the sofa when I got back to the office. What a little cutie! He looked so peaceful. There was no sign of Socks. Winky's flags were on the windowsill. Maybe he'd been giving Socks semaphore lessons?

I glanced across the street, and saw Bella in her window. Maybe she was looking for Winky? Perhaps I should wake him; he'd be disappointed if he missed her.

"Winky!" He didn't stir.

I glanced again at Bella. This time, there was another cat sidling up to her. Oh dear, Winky wouldn't be happy.

"What's all the noise about?" Winky yawned.

I looked back at Bella, and that's when I recognised the other cat. It was Socks—he and Bella seemed to be very friendly.

"What are you staring at?" Winky said. "Is Bella there?"

"Err—Bella? Your girlfriend? Err—No. There's definitely

no Bella over there."

"Are you sure? She said she'd be there later."

"No. Definitely no Bella."

He got up. "Move out of the way. Let me have a look."

"Pardon?"

"Come on. You heard me—move out of the way."

I picked up his flags, and held them out to him. "Why don't you show me some semaphore?"

"Have you gone crazy, woman? Get out of my way."

Oh well. I'd tried. I stepped to one side, and Winky jumped into the windowsill. Any second now, he'd go ballistic.

"Bella gets more beautiful every day." He sighed.

Huh? I turned around, and looked back across at Bella's window. Socks had disappeared; Bella was all alone. Phew!

"Where's your brother, Winky?"

"He's gone to catch up with some old friends. He's such a great guy, don't you think?"

"Oh, yeah. He's a great guy all right."

***

I heard movement in the outer office, and assumed it was a delivery of some kind. But then, I caught a whiff of something. It wasn't an unpleasant smell; in fact, it was really rather nice. Floral. Curiosity eventually got the better of me, so I went to investigate.

Every surface of Mrs V's office was covered with flowers. Dozens of bouquets of every colour and type of flower imaginable. I could barely see her at her desk, until I popped my head through the foliage.

"Mrs V? What's going on? I know business is slow, but you really should have consulted me before opening a flower shop out here."

She looked as confused as I was.

"A delivery man came up to the office about thirty minutes ago. He said he had some flowers for me. I thought it might have been a 'thank you' from G. He brought up four bouquets to begin with, but then he brought more and more until I ended up with this lot. I told him it must be a mistake, and that he must have the wrong name or address. But he checked his paperwork, and said they were for Annabel Versailles, care of this office."

"Who sent them?"

"I don't know. They all have the same printed card with them."

I picked out the card from the bouquet closest to me. On it was printed: *'To Annabel. Please be mine. Yours, Armi.'*

"Armi? Who's Armi?"

She shook her head. "I don't know. Unless—"

"No!" I said. "Surely it can't be Gordon Armitage?"

"I hope not." She looked horrified at the thought.

"Have you been flirting with him, Mrs V?"

"Of course not. How could you suggest such a thing? I can't stand that obnoxious man."

"What are you going to do with this lot?"

"I can't keep them. They'll set my hay fever off. I've been in touch with Yarnie Relief."

"What's that?"

"A charity which supports those injured in the course of knitting. They run a market stall every day. They're going to send someone around to collect them in the next few minutes. They may as well be sold to raise some money for a good cause."

"Okay, I'll leave you to it."

As I walked back to my office, I sang, "Gordon and Annabel sitting in a tree—"

"Jill! I have some very sharp knitting needles, and I'm not afraid to use them."

***

I'd just arrived back at my block of flats when Kathy called.

"Have you seen The Bugle today?"

"No, you know I hate that rag."

"I think you'll want to see this. Take a look at the full page ad on page thirty-six."

"What is it?"

"It's an ad for a new P.I. business. Looks like you've got competition. Sorry, I have to go. Pete's dinner is going to burn."

I needed to check this out, so I dashed over to the newsagent to pick up a copy of The Bugle. Surprisingly, Jasper James *wasn't* behind the counter.

"Where's Jasper today?" I asked the young man who appeared to be standing in for him.

"Dad? He's at a conference: Fedora World."

Of course he was.

As soon as I got back to my flat, I flicked through to page thirty-six. Sure enough, there was the full page ad that Kathy had mentioned.

The headline read: *'Don't Settle For Good(er). Demand The Best. Best P.I. Services. Now Open In Washbridge'.*

I had no problem with fair competition. There'd always been other private investigators in Washbridge. But there was no need for a disparaging advert like that. *'Don't settle for gooder'*? That was obviously targeted at me.

I'd have to take a closer look at this new competitor.

Chapter 11

Overnight, I decided I'd have to speak to Socks. I couldn't allow him to treat his brother like that.

As I made the short walk from my car to the office, I noticed people handing out flyers outside my building. They were probably for another new pizza place, so I grabbed one as I walked by, just in case there were any opening offers.

What the? How dare they?

The flyer was for Best P.I. Services, and it had the same heading as the advert in The Bugle: *'Don't Settle For Good(er)'*. The audacity! To hand these out right outside my door!

"Have you seen those people outside, Mrs V?"

"With the flyers? Yes, they gave me one."

"I can't believe their cheek."

"That's not the worst of it, dear."

"What do you mean?"

"Have you been listening to Radio Washbridge?"

"No, I never listen to the radio in the morning."

"They're running an ad every fifteen minutes for Best P.I. Services."

This was war!

I didn't want Winky to overhear me talking to Socks, so I waited until my one-eyed darling was asleep. His despicable brother was sitting on my desk doing something on his smartphone.

"Hey, Socks! You and I need to have words."

"What's got you so riled up, little witchy? Winky told me you had a hot temper."

"Don't '*little witchy*' me."

"Look, I know I dropped in kind of unannounced, but it's not my fault my bro didn't give you fair warning."

"It's got nothing to do with that." I glanced across at Winky to make sure he hadn't stirred. "I *saw* you!"

"I saw you too, girl. And, you're pretty hot for a witch."

"Never mind all the flannel. I saw you across the way with Bella."

"That Bella is one hot pussycat."

"She's Winky's girlfriend!"

"Him and me are bros. What's his is mine, and what's mine is his."

"That does *not* extend to his girlfriend."

"Chillax! There's plenty of Miss Bella to go around."

"Do you think Winky will agree when I tell him?"

"You wouldn't do that."

"Try me."

"Okay, okay. If it makes you happy, I'll leave the lady alone."

Winky stirred. "What are you two talking about?"

"Witchy here was just asking me which salmon I preferred." Socks winked at me.

"Need you ask." Winky jumped off the sofa. "Red not pink, obviously."

***

Grandma dropped into the office—unannounced. This was getting to be a habit.

"How's the filming going?" I asked.

"They're not giving enough attention to the Everlasting Wool and One-Size Knitting Needles."

"It's not supposed to be an advert."

"See? This is why your business never has any clients. You fail to grasp even the basics of marketing."

"To what do I owe the pleasure of your company, Grandma?"

"I understand you're wasting your time with this wand nonsense?"

"By *wand nonsense*, I assume you mean the Wand of Magna? Yes, Aunt Lucy asked if I'd help with the investigation."

"A lot of fuss over nothing." She scoffed.

"But surely it's part of the rich history of witchcraft?"

"Baloney! I was on level four when Magna Mondale was made the first ever level six witch. She was magnificent. There's never been anyone like her, before or since. But, I can tell you this for nothing—she wouldn't have wanted all this fuss about her wand. When she became a level six witch, the first thing she did was to discard it, and she encouraged other witches to do the same. So, why would anyone preserve it as though it's an important exhibit? That thing should be broken into pieces and burned. Did Coral Fish mention the sealed room to you?"

"She did, yes. It's Magna Mondale's original basement, isn't it?"

"Yes. Magna developed spells that others hadn't even dreamed of—they were so powerful that she feared what might happen if they fell into the wrong hands. If they'd been used for evil, it would have been devastating for Candlefield. When she knew she was dying, she sealed them away in that room. No one has been able to get in there since."

"Have you ever tried to get in there, Grandma?"

"No. Of course not."

There was something in her response which made me wonder if she was being entirely honest.

"If I was you, I'd drop this case."

"I can't do that now. I've already promised Aunt Lucy I would help."

"To find a worthless wand? What's the point?"

"The point is that I've given my word. I don't intend to go back on it."

"Very noble, I'm sure."

"Is that the only reason you came to see me?" I couldn't hide my annoyance. I was even more determined than ever to find the wand now.

"Actually, no. I wanted to tell you that the team photo for The Candle is tomorrow afternoon. We're meeting at The Candle's offices at four o' clock."

"What if I'm busy then?"

"Get un-busy."

***

It was time to pay another visit to Mad in prison.

As I was walking down the stairs from my office, I heard footsteps behind me. It was the funny little man—the one who'd been talking to Gordon Armitage. I thought no more about it, and carried on out of the building and down the street towards my car. But after a couple of minutes, I realised the funny little man was still behind me.

Was this Armitage's latest attempt to spy on me? If so, the guy he'd hired wasn't very good at his job. I needed to be sure, so I took four left turns, and ended up back where I started. He was still behind me.

It was time to have words with my funny little friend.

"What do you think you're doing? Why are you following me? If you're a P.I, I have to tell you, you're pretty useless."

The man looked terrified. "I'm not a P.I."

"But you *are* following me, so I assume you're working for Gordon Armitage."

"No, I'm not. I mean—I *was* following you, but I'm not doing it for Gordon."

"Why then?"

"I didn't know what else to do. I think the way Gordon has treated you and Annabel is appalling."

"Annabel? Do you know Mrs V?"

"Yes. Well, no. Not really."

"Now I'm confused. What do you want? Do you work for Gordon Armitage or not?"

"Not exactly."

This man was trying my patience. "*What* exactly, then?"

"I'm one of the partners at Armitage, Armitage, Armitage and Poole. I'm Joseph—"

"Poole?"

"No. Joseph Armitage. I'm Gordon's brother. His older brother."

"You're not the least bit alike."

"Thank goodness for that." He gave a nervous laugh.

"Wait a minute," I said. "You're not—did you send—are you Armi?"

He blushed.

"Oh wow! So you're Mrs V's secret admirer!"

"Did she like the flowers?"

"I think you may have overdone it a tad."

"Oh dear."

"Do you actually know Mrs V? Have you ever spoken to her?"

"No, I've just admired her from a distance. I thought the flowers might be an ice-breaker."

"Would you like to meet her?"

"That would be great."

"Leave it with me, Armi. I'll see what I can do."

***

I'd expected Mad to be really down in the dumps, but surprisingly she was much brighter than the last time I'd seen her. The orange jumpsuit did nothing for her.

"How's it going, Mad?"

"I've had better times."

"Are they treating you all right? How's the food?"

"It's better than the slop my mother serves up."

"Has she been to see you yet?"

"Not yet. She reckons visiting time clashes with her bingo."

"Surely visiting her daughter in prison is more important than bingo?"

"That's what I said, but apparently the regional flyer is set to pay out a record jackpot, and she doesn't want to miss out on it." Mad rolled her eyes. "Have you made any progress with the investigation?"

"So far, the only real lead I've got is the CCTV footage. I counted everyone who went in and out of the building on the day of the murder. If my calculations are correct, one person was still in the library after the doors were locked."

"You actually sat and counted them all? That must have been mind-numbingly boring."

"It was, but I've become immune to boredom since living next door to Mr Ivers."

"Who?"

"Never mind. I've got someone going through the footage again to see if they can identify the individual who stayed behind."

"I really appreciate all your help, Jill."

"Have you heard any more from the police?"

"I have, and it isn't good. It seems they found my fingerprints on the knife that killed Anita."

"Did they show you the knife?"

"Only a photo."

"Did you recognise it?"

"Yes, but it isn't mine."

"How come your fingerprints are on it, then?"

"Do you remember I told you Anita and I had been at a fundraiser on the night before she was murdered?"

"Yeah."

"It was in aid of the Carnation Foundation. The knife used to kill Anita was one of the steak knives from that event. I remember because they had a distinctive blue handle. Someone must have taken my knife after I'd used it."

"Did you tell the police that?"

"Of course, but I'm not sure they were listening. They seem to have made their minds up already."

We talked for about another hour, and then I left with the promise that I'd keep her updated. I needed to find out more about the fundraiser, and in particular about the Carnation Foundation.

***

First though, it was time to check out 'Best P.I. Services'. Time to find out exactly who the competition was. According to the address on the flyers, their offices were only a short walk from my own. The building in which they were located was relatively new. Inside, was a huge reception area which served all of the offices in the building. The man behind the reception desk directed me to the seventh floor.

Once there, I spotted a red sign with the words, 'Best P.I. Services'. Inside was a very professional-looking receptionist who was busy on her computer—there wasn't a knitting needle or crochet hook in sight. I was pretty sure that her CV wouldn't include stints in the food packing industry.

"Good morning, madam. Do you have an appointment?"

"No. But I'd like to see whoever's in charge here, please."

"I'll have to see if anyone is available. What's your name, please?"

"Jill Gooder."

"Will you take a seat please, madam?"

The leather sofa squeaked as I sat down; it still smelled very new. In fact, everything about the office looked sparkly and new.

"There's a lady in reception who'd like to see you. Her name is Jill Gooder. Yes, very well."

"You can go through." She pointed at the door to her right.

I walked through into a larger office, which again was beautifully decorated with expensive-looking furniture. On the far side of the room was a desk. Behind it, sat a man with his back to me. He seemed to be studying the wall for some reason. As I walked towards him, he suddenly swivelled around in his chair.

"Miles?"

He grinned.

"Since when were you a private investigator?"

"Since yesterday actually. Have you seen the ads?"

"Yes, I've seen the *ads*. They're downright despicable. What do you mean by, *'better than Gooder'*?"

"It's just marketing, Jill. Nothing personal. Surely you're not afraid of a little competition?"

"How are you even qualified to be a private investigator?"

He pointed to a framed certificate on the wall next to him.

"Just a minute. This says, 'Awarded by the Best School for Private Investigators'. You issued this to yourself!"

He shrugged. "How is that any different to you? Weren't you taught by Daddy?"

It took all of my self-control not to pull him across the desk, and strangle him.

"Where's Mindy? Is she skulking around here somewhere, too?"

"Mindy's looking after Best Wool today."

"Well, Miles, I can't stop you setting up as a private investigator, but you'd better stop handing out flyers right outside my building or there'll be trouble."

"Very touchy, aren't we? Just like your cousins. It seems no one in your family can handle a little competition."

I had to leave before I did something I'd regret. I'd never been fond of Miles, but I'd always been able to hold it in check. Until now. Now the gloves were off!

Chapter 12

"Have you had any more flowers from Gordon, Mrs V?"

"I suppose you think that's funny, Jill."

"What would you say if I told you I know who your secret admirer really is?"

"Do you?"

"I might."

"Who is it?"

"I'm not sure I should tell you."

"Have you forgotten that I have sharp knitting needles in the drawer?"

"Okay. It turns out that Gordon Armitage has an older brother named Joseph. He followed me out into the street. I thought he'd been hired by Gordon to check up on me, but when I confronted him, it turned out that he actually has the hots for you."

Mrs V blushed. "Don't be silly."

"It's true. He's very shy—he thought the flowers might break the ice."

"He rather overdid it, didn't he?"

"That's what I told him. Anyway, he said he'd love to meet up with you."

"You mean, like a date?"

"I guess so."

"I'm too old for dating."

"You're never too old, Mrs V. Shall I tell him yes?"

"I don't suppose it would do any harm."

Jill Gooder, matchmaker extraordinaire, strikes again.

***

It wasn't difficult to find information about the Carnation Foundation. It appeared to be some kind of 'umbrella' organisation which specialised in raising funds for a number of animal and children's charities. Their website and brochure made very interesting reading. One of the patrons was none other than Gregory Pick.

But, even more interesting, was an article in The Bugle, which covered the fundraising event which Mad had attended. The person who had organised it was Gregory Pick's new girlfriend, Lily Bell. Apparently, he'd been out of the country playing golf on the night of the fundraiser, but Lily Bell had been in attendance.

That information immediately moved Lily Bell up a few notches on my list of people of interest. It was quite likely that she would have been involved in compiling the guest list for the function, and she would have had an opportunity to take the knife from Madeline's table.

It turned out that the Carnation Foundation had a local office, which was only a couple of streets away from Ever A Wool Moment. On the off chance, I took a walk over there. It was an inauspicious building, and only a very small office. I went inside with the intention of speaking to whoever I found there. To my surprise, it was Lily Bell. She stared at me for a moment with a puzzled expression—she was obviously trying to work out how she knew me. Then it must have clicked.

"You're that private detective woman, aren't you?"

"That's right. Jill Gooder."

"What are you doing here?"

"I was hoping to talk to someone about the Carnation Foundation."

"You'd better come through to the back, then."

She led me to an even smaller office, which contained a single desk and two chairs. Lily Bell was glammed up to the nines in designer clothes, and looked rather out of place in such a tacky little office.

"What exactly would you like to know?"

"I understand you had a fundraising event the other night."

"We did. I was the organiser and chairperson."

"So I read. Did Gregory appoint you to the position?"

"What if he did? My track record speaks for itself. We're on target to raise record funds this year."

"Did the evening go well?"

"Yes, it was a runaway success. We raised a lot of money, and raised awareness too."

"I understand Anita Pick was at the fundraiser. Did you invite her?"

"I most certainly did not!" She looked horrified at the idea. "I'm not sure what she was doing there. I can't imagine how she or her little friend managed to get hold of the tickets. Those tickets were like gold dust. She probably stole them, knowing Anita." Lily Bell seemed to realise what she'd just said. "But one shouldn't speak ill of the dead, I suppose."

"Do you have a list of all the people who had access to the invitations?"

"That would be just the committee members." She pulled open a drawer, and handed me a sheet of headed paper. "They're all listed on there."

"Roxy Blackwall?"

"Yes. Do you know her?"

"Not really. We've only met the once."

"She's dedicated, but only really interested in the animal

charities. She's not really a 'people' person."

Lily Bell and I talked for almost thirty minutes about the foundation and her role in it. To my surprise, she seemed to have a genuine passion for the charities, and for the part she played. This seemed to fly in the face of the image that had been painted of her, by Anita's solicitor, as a money-grabbing gold digger.

Would the real Lily Bell please stand up?

**

Mrs V had asked if she could bring her small, portable TV to work, so she could watch the Wool TV reality show, Wool Shop Yarns. I didn't see any reason to object. It wasn't as though we were overrun with clients.

She suddenly came rushing into my office.

"Jill! Quick! Come and look at this."

"What is it, Mrs V? I'm rather busy." That made Winky laugh for some reason.

"You'll want to see this. Hurry up!"

I followed her into the outer office, where she pointed to the TV.

"Just look at this."

It was Wool Shop Yarns, and the camera was focused on Kathy and Grandma who were behind the counter. Kathy looked extremely flustered; Grandma just looked angry. Very angry! The wart on her nose was glowing red, which was never a good sign.

"What's going on, Mrs V?"

"Just keep watching."

When the camera pulled back, I could see four or five women at the other side of the counter. They were all waving their arms around, and were obviously unhappy about something.

"Turn it up, Mrs V. I can't hear it."

"This is meant to be Everlasting Wool!" one of the women shouted. "So why has mine run out?"

"There's a perfectly reasonable explanation," Grandma said.

"Yes, there is." One of the other women interrupted. "It sucks! I was halfway through a cardigan, which I was knitting for my niece's birthday, and it just ran out. I rang the Everlasting Wool support line, but the woman on there was next to useless."

Kathy seemed to be studying her feet. One of her jobs was to man the support line. The problem was, she had no more idea how Everlasting Wool worked than the women who were calling in for help.

I'd thought Grandma had resolved the problems with Everlasting Wool, but obviously not all of them.

"So what are you going to do about it?" a third woman demanded. "Look at this scarf. It's only two-thirds finished. I can't match this colour anywhere else. I need my subscription to start working again."

"It's all in hand, madam." Grandma kept glancing directly into the lens of the camera. She knew this was being broadcast live. Instead of being the advertisement she'd been hoping for, this was turning into a P.R. disaster.

"*When* will it get sorted?" one of the women said.

"By the end of today, all the subscriptions will be working again." Grandma reassured them.

"It better had or we'll be back here again tomorrow."

Talk about train wreck TV.

***

There was no sign of Socks in the office.

"Has your brother gone back home?"

"Socks? No, he'll be here for a while yet."

"Where is he?"

"My bro doesn't hang around. He's found himself a girlfriend already. Poor girl, little does she know he likes to love 'em and leave 'em. Still, they'll have fun together while he's up here."

"Do you know anything about his new girlfriend?"

"Not really. He said she's a bit of a looker, but then all of his girlfriends are hot."

"All?"

"He's always been a bit of a ladies' man."

I bet he has.

"I was actually a bit jealous of him when I was growing up," Winky said. "Not now of course. Not now I have Bella."

Oh dear. I was beginning to think my chat with Socks hadn't done any good. I wandered casually over to the window, and glanced across the way. There was no sign of Bella. Had she gone out somewhere with Socks? Should I tell Winky what was going on? But what if Socks had given up on Bella? What if he'd found himself another girlfriend? Winky and his brother were obviously very close. I didn't want to do anything which would damage their relationship until I was absolutely sure.

"Did Socks say he'd bring his girlfriend over to meet you?"

"It's funny you should ask that. He usually likes to show off his ladies, but this time, he didn't seem very keen."

I bet he didn't.

I'd completely underestimated the number of phone calls I'd get as a result of the BoundBall piece in The Candle. The article itself was a travesty. Don Roming had basically tried to turn the whole thing into some kind of a joke; he'd mocked the very idea of women playing BoundBall. That obnoxious man had now joined Dougal Bugle on my list of journalists to avoid.

Despite the disparaging article, I'd had calls from dozens of women—all keen to take part in the game. I had been worried that I wouldn't be able to recruit enough players, but I'd actually ended up with far too many. I was starting to get excited about the whole venture.

I'd told everyone who called, to meet me in Candlefield Park, after work. It was a cold, damp evening, and I was a little concerned the weather might put a few people off, but I needn't have worried. Thirty-one women turned up; a mixture of all kinds of sups.

"Hi everyone. For those of you who don't already know me, I'm Jill Gooder. This game was my idea, and I'm thrilled to see so many of you here today. Let's have a show of hands—how many of you have actually played BoundBall before?"

To my amazement and delight, every one of them raised a hand.

One of the women at the front, a witch, stepped forward.

"My name's Anthea Close."

"Hi, Anthea."

"Hi. A lot of women play BoundBall. Okay, it's only a fraction of the number of men who play, but we're just as passionate about it as they are. We have our own league, although you'd never know it because it gets no coverage in the press. But then, what would you expect? All the sports reporters are men."

Everyone nodded; a few laughed.

"We've wanted an opportunity like this for years," she continued. "Something that would raise the profile of the women's game, but the men would never entertain the idea of playing against a women's team."

"Well, you're going to get your chance now. I assume you know how this all came about?"

"It's for SupAid, isn't it?"

"Yes, and we mustn't forget that's the main reason we're doing this. It's a great cause, but at the moment they're struggling for donations. This tournament should help them in a big way." I hesitated. "But we're also in it to win it!"

Everyone cheered.

"There is just one thing we need to clear up, Jill," Anthea said.

"What's that?"

"I don't really know how to say this, but we don't think you should play in the team."

That was music to my ears, but I waited for her to continue.

"As far as we're aware, you've never played BoundBall."

"You're right. I haven't. That's absolutely fine by me. I was prepared to play if we couldn't make the numbers, but I'd much rather field a team of experienced players. And if everyone here agrees, why don't you be the captain?"

Everyone seemed to like that idea.

"I'd be honoured." Anthea beamed with obvious pride.

"In that case, you can pick the team, and I'll just watch from the sideline."

"You have to be our manager," Anthea said.

"I'll do it—if everyone agrees."

Anthea turned to the others. "All those who want Jill to be our manager, say 'Aye'."

It was unanimous.

"Thank you, everyone." I was a little overwhelmed. "Anthea—if you could organise the practice sessions and select the team, that would be fantastic."

"I'll be happy to. There is just one other thing—what do we call ourselves? We all play for different teams. We'll need a new name for this particular game."

I thought about it for a moment. "Why not just call ourselves 'W'?"

"Yeah 'W'!" Everyone agreed. "Go 'W'!"

Chapter 13

Mr Ivers looked down in the dumps. As a caring neighbour, I should have enquired if he was okay, and asked if there was anything I could do to help. *Alternatively,* I could have hidden behind a tree, and hoped he didn't see me.

Whoops! Too late. He was headed my way.

"Morning, Mr Ivers."

"Morning, Jill," he grunted.

For a moment, I wondered if Alicia still had her claws into him. But his eyes were clear, and he was responding. He did look incredibly sad though.

"Is everything okay?" What was I doing? Why didn't I just keep walking? I was getting soft in my old age.

"Not really. I'm rather sad." Never had a truer word been spoken.

"Why's that, Mr Ivers?" See how I made it sound like I cared. Oscar material.

"You met Tess, didn't you?"

"Oh yes. I met her."

"I thought we were getting on really well, but then something seemed to go wrong."

Poisoning your partner can have that effect.

"Wrong how?"

"I honestly don't know. It all started when I became ill – I must have caught the flu or something."

Definitely *or something.*

"I wasn't myself for a couple of days; I felt completely out of it. But then, I seemed to shake it off. After that, though, Tess wouldn't come anywhere near me. It was as if she was afraid of catching something."

"I'm a little like that myself. I stay away from my nephew and niece when they're ill." Or too noisy.

"Every time Tess tried to get close to me, it was as if something held her back."

The 'wicked witch away' spell had obviously worked.

"And then, out of the blue, she said we were finished."

"Did you ask her why?"

"Of course! I asked if I'd done something wrong. I told her I could change, and that I'd do anything to keep us together. She just said it wasn't me it was her."

If I had a pound for every time I'd heard that.

"She said she couldn't be near me anymore."

"I'm sorry to hear that, Mr Ivers. But there are plenty more fish in the sea."

"Not like Tess. We were made for one another. She was my angel."

Angel of death, more like.

I knew how I could cheer him up. I would offer to go on a date with him.

What? Of course I wasn't being serious. But, be honest, I had you fooled there for a minute, didn't I?

***

Mrs V seemed unusually chipper. She was obviously very pleased with herself about something.

"You look very happy with life, Mrs V. What's going on?"

"Nothing." She blushed.

"I don't believe you. Come on. You can tell me."

"Well, if you must know, I went out with Armi last night."

"On a date? You sly, old thing. You never mentioned

anything about it to me, yesterday."

"My love life is my own business. I don't enquire into yours."

"Yes you do. All the time."

"That's different."

Obviously.

"So? How did it go? I want all the sordid details."

"There are no sordid details. Armi was the perfect gentleman."

"Pretty boring, then?"

"Not in the least. He took me to dinner at his club."

"Ooh, very fancy!"

"It's a private members club. Very nice it is, too. Very upmarket. The food was absolutely delicious. Apparently, the chef used to work in one of the top hotels in France."

"Really? So what did you have? Fish fingers and chips?"

"I had the duck." She was a past master at ignoring my facetiousness.

"Come on, then. Spill the beans. What's he like? Hopefully he doesn't take after his brother."

"He's nothing like that horrible Gordon Armitage, thank goodness. It's hard to believe they're brothers. We didn't talk about work, or Gordon, or anything like that. Armi was very good company — very interesting to talk to. A little shy, but he seemed keen to know all about me. He asked about my interests and hobbies and so on. He even offered me free legal advice."

"That was nice of him."

"That's what I thought. Apparently he specialises in Wills."

Alarm bells started to ring. Was Armi actually the goblin that Daze had told me about?

I was hoping to hear back from my CCTV guy, Simon Saize, at any time. If, as I suspected, the person who had stayed behind in the library turned out to be Lily Bell, I'd have enough to take it to Jack Maxwell. She'd been in charge of the invitations, which meant she could have ensured both Anita and Mad were at the fundraiser. And, she'd had the opportunity to take Mad's knife. Lily Bell certainly had the motive. She was a gold digger if ever there was one, and she obviously hated the idea of Anita taking what she probably perceived as *her* money.

As soon as I got the call, I hurried over to the security company.

Simon Saize fast forwarded the tape to two p.m.

"That's the woman." He pointed. "She never came out."

I was expecting to see the tall, striking figure of Lily Bell. Instead, I saw a short, squat woman, over a foot shorter. The woman had a large bag over her shoulder, and was wearing a hat, which when combined with the sunglasses, obscured her face. It was impossible to identify her.

I now had an image of the murderer, but I was no closer to knowing who she was. The only thing I knew for sure was that it was not Lily Bell.

I was back to square one.

***

I needed a blueberry muffin, and I knew just the place where I would get a staff discount—one hundred per cent discount, if I had anything to do with it.

What? Of course it isn't theft. It's a perk of the job.

"It's not on!" Amber protested.

"It shouldn't be allowed!" Pearl said.

"Sorry, girls. It's only the one muffin. I didn't think you'd mind."

"We're not talking about you," Amber said.

"Yeah, we're used to your thieving ways." Pearl managed a half-smile.

"What's wrong, then?"

"What do you think? Miles Best."

"Don't mention that man to me!" I said.

The twins seemed taken aback by my reaction.

"What's he done to *you*?" Pearl asked.

"I'll tell you in a minute. First, what's he done to upset the two of you, this time?"

"It's just not fair," Amber said. "He comes out smelling of roses every time."

"How do you mean?"

"Look over there." She pointed across the road. Best Cakes was full of customers; in stark contrast to Cuppy C.

"It's all the publicity from the clown infestation." Pearl sighed. "It worked wonders for his business, so now they have a different circus theme every day."

"Oh dear. Your revenge kind of backfired, didn't it?"

"No need to rub it in," Amber said. "It seemed like a good idea at the time."

"What theme is it today? I can't see from here."

"I sneaked over there earlier," Pearl said. "It's tightrope walker day. There are two of them. One in the cake shop, and one in the tea room. It seems to be very popular; the place is buzzing."

"How are you going to compete with that?" I asked.

"Don't worry, Jill." Pearl smiled. "We have a cunning plan."

Oh dear.

"We're going to host a different craft exhibition each day."

Underwhelmed didn't cover it.

"That's not quite as exciting as circus acts though, is it?"

"Of course it is." Amber insisted. "We've got the first one lined up already: pottery."

"Pottery? He's got clowns, fire eaters and tightrope walkers—and you've got *pottery*?"

"It'll be great," Pearl said.

"Yeah, can't wait." Yawn.

"So, what has Miles done to upset *you*, Jill?" Amber said.

"He's only gone and set up in competition with me, as a private investigator."

"In Washbridge?"

"Yeah, he's calling himself Best P.I. Services. First, he targets you with Best Cakes, then he targets Grandma with Best Wool, and now he has the audacity to target me with Best P.I. Services! You should see the ads he's running. He had a full-page advert in The Bugle. And he had people standing outside my office, handing out fliers."

"The cheek of the man!" Pearl shook her head.

"You haven't heard the best, yet. He's also running adverts on Radio Washbridge. All of his ads say the same thing: *'Don't settle for Gooder, get the Best'*."

"That is funny." Pearl laughed.

"No, it isn't!"

"Sorry, you're right. It isn't. Not at all."

"What are you going to do about it?" Amber asked.

"I went to see him. He has a really posh office in the centre of town. I don't know how long he'll be able to pay for that. And, he'll get no change out of Jack Maxwell. Jack can't stand private investigators. When he first came here, he made it very difficult for me, but now he and I have an understanding."

"Hmm, so I heard." Amber grinned.

"Not *that* kind of understanding. Jack respects me as a professional. He knows that I want to work *with* him. Miles Best would have to work very hard to earn that kind of respect. I can't see him doing that. I give him three months at the most."

"Well?" Grandma came bursting through the doors—she was waving something in her hand. "Let's hear it?"

I glanced around, wondering who she was talking to. Somehow the twins had disappeared; they were probably hiding behind the counter.

"Are you talking to me, Grandma?"

"Of course I'm talking to you!" She was holding a newspaper, which she spread out on the nearest table. "Notice anything missing?"

It took me a few moments to realise what she was referring to, but then I spotted the photograph.

Oh bum!

"I'm so sorry, Grandma. I forgot all about it."

"How many times did I remind you about the Compass team photograph?"

"I—err."

"Ten, that's how many."

That was an outright lie, but now wasn't the time to

correct her.

"I'm sorry. I was so busy, I totally forgot."

"You made me look a fool." Her wart was already at DefCon two.

"I'm really, really sorry."

"I don't know why I bother!" She turned and stormed out.

"Forget something, Jill?" Amber poked her head above the counter.

"Say cheese." Pearl giggled.

I threw what was left of my muffin at them.

***

I don't know why I allowed myself to get involved; I should have kept my nose out. Call me a big softy, but I couldn't bear to think of Bella cheating on Winky. Now, it's true that Winky had his shortcomings—if you have a couple of days free sometime, I'll list them all—but I'd take him any day of the week over his brother, Socks. What a despicable character he'd turned out to be.

I had thought that my little *chat* with Socks had warned him off, but it was obvious that he'd taken no notice whatsoever. Enough was enough. I had to put an end to this, but I was going to need proof because Winky thought the sun shone out of Socks'—you get my drift. Winky wasn't simply going to take my word for it that his brother was seeing Bella. He'd think I was crazy or that I was making it up just to get rid of Socks. I needed photographic evidence of the two of them together.

I couldn't let Winky know what I was up to, so every now and then, I would walk nonchalantly over to the window, and pretend to look out at the street below.

"What's up with you, today?" he said.

"Nothing, why?"

"That's the tenth time you've been to that window in the last two hours."

I shrugged.

"You're up to something. You never look out the window."

"I just realised that I don't appreciate this view enough."

"What view? There is no view. You're cracking up, if you ask me."

I ignored his remark, and continued to make regular checks to see if Bella was in her window, and more specifically, if Socks was with her.

Eventually, I struck lucky. The two of them were sidling up to one another in the window opposite. Luckily, Winky hadn't seen them; he was fast asleep. This was my opportunity.

I sneaked out of the room as quietly as I could. I didn't want to risk waking him.

"I'm nipping out for a few minutes, Mrs V."

"Okay, dear."

"Don't go into my office. Winky is asleep, and I wouldn't want you to wake him."

She gave me a puzzled look. "Okay, Jill, but it's not as though I ever go in there willingly. The less contact I have with that stupid cat, the better."

I hurried outside, and across the road to the building where Bella lived. The last time I'd been there was to drop flowers off for her birthday. This time, I actually needed to get inside if I was going to get my photograph.

I knocked on the door, and immediately made myself

invisible.

"Hello? Hello?" The man who came to the door looked understandably confused.

When he stepped out into the corridor, I slipped past him. Once inside, I quickly found the room where Bella and Socks were still smooching in the windowsill. Although I was angry primarily with Socks, Bella was just as much to blame. She should be ashamed of herself for two-timing Winky like that.

I took out my phone, and snapped a couple of photos of them, and then made my way out. I knocked on the door again — from the inside this time. The man re-appeared — chuntering to himself.

"Those stupid kids are at it again. I should call the police on them."

When he opened the door, I once again slipped past him, and made my getaway.

I now had the evidence I needed, but how was I going to break it to Winky? I'd sleep on it, and then pick my moment the following day.

Chapter 14

The next morning, I still wasn't feeling any better about what I had to do. Not only was this going to ruin Winky's relationship with his brother, but it would probably also signal the end for him and Bella.

"By the way." Winky jumped onto my desk. "Did I mention that Socks is going to be staying for another two weeks?"

"No, you didn't. I'm sorry, but that's not convenient."

"But you can't send my bro away. It's not like he visits very often."

"Too often," I said under my breath.

"Pardon?"

"I can't have two cats in the office. It's bad enough with one."

"What am I meant to do for company? I'm by myself all the time. I never see another cat."

Was that a violin I could hear?

"Do me a favour. You run the semaphore classes. You get to see plenty of other cats at those. And it isn't all that long ago since you were posing as Madame Winkesca, and fleecing cats out of their—I mean, telling their fortunes. You see plenty of cats."

"But they're not family. Socks is the only family I have now. Surely you understand that. I know how important family is to you."

"Trust me, Winky, you're better off without him."

"How can you say that about my bro? I don't insult your sister, and she's always coming around here. It's only for another two weeks."

"Winky, I didn't want to tell you this, but—"

"But what? What lame excuse are you going to come up with now?"

"If I tell you, you have to promise not to get upset."

"Upset about what? You're talking in riddles as per usual."

"Socks has been seeing Bella."

He laughed. "Is that the best you can come up with? Really, Jill, I'm disappointed in you. Of all the lies you could have dreamed up to try to persuade me to get rid of Socks, you thought I'd believe that load of old rubbish? Bella and I are an item. She only has eyes for me, and besides, my bro would never do something like that to me."

I held out my smartphone.

"What's that?"

"Take a look."

Winky stared in disbelief.

"I'm sorry, Winky, I really didn't want to show you."

"I'm going to kill him."

"There's no need for violence."

"He's a dead cat walking."

"You mustn't overreact."

"When did you take these photos?"

"Yesterday."

"And you've only just told me?"

"I was waiting for the right moment."

"Where is he now?"

"I don't know."

"Is he with Bella?"

"I don't know. I haven't seen either of them this morning."

"I'm going over there."

"No, you mustn't. If you make a scene, Bella's owners will call the cat pound, and you'll be locked up. Wait until he comes back, and then have a quiet word."

"A quiet word? Are you kidding? There'll be no words of the quiet variety. When he gets back here, he'll wish he'd never been born."

Oh bum!

**

I was still mulling over the CCTV coverage. Although Simon Saize had identified the image of the person who had stayed behind in the library, it hadn't helped. The hat and sunglasses had meant it was impossible to identify the individual.

But then, something occurred to me. Simon had studied the CCTV between the time the doors opened, and the time they were locked again. What about the period of time *after* the doors were locked? The murderer must have made her getaway somehow, otherwise the police would have found her when they took Mad in for questioning.

I contacted Simon to ask if I could take one last look at the footage. He agreed, so I went straight over there. After he'd set me up in the same room as on my previous visit, I fast-forwarded to the point where the doors were locked. Nothing happened for a while, but then suddenly the flashing lights of a police vehicle were visible. The library doors opened—I assumed Mad must have unlocked them—and the police went inside. A few moments later, someone else left the building. It was a paramedic.

Hold on. How was that possible? There'd been no sign of the paramedics arriving. I went to get Simon, and asked if he could zoom in on the paramedic, so I could get a closer look. He did, but it was hopeless; the picture was too fuzzy to see any detail. I was pretty sure it was a woman though. She was the same height and build as the person who had stayed behind. Now, at least, I knew how she'd made her getaway. She must have changed into the paramedic's uniform after she'd murdered Anita Pick, and waited until the emergency services arrived. Then, she was able to walk casually out of the building—no one would have thought to question a paramedic.

Now, everything made sense.

I drove to Anita Pick's house, and went next door. The dogs were barking, but they were locked in the back yard, so I wasn't worried. Roxy Blackwall answered the door.

"You again? More questions?"

"A few, yes. How long have you been on the organising committee of the Carnation Foundation?"

"Three years. They do an excellent job. Anything to do with dogs, and you can count me in. How did you know?"

"I've been doing some checking into the foundation. I was particularly interested in the fundraising evening they held the other night. I imagine you're able to get hold of extra invitations to those sorts of events?"

"Yes, a few."

"And I assume you passed two of those invitations on to your neighbour, and her colleague from the library?"

"I don't know what you're talking about. I wouldn't give Anita Pick the time of day, let alone an invitation to a fundraiser."

"I think you did. You probably told her it was a peace offering, but really you still wanted revenge for Jo Jo. And how better to cover your tracks, than to frame someone else for the murder? The ideal candidate was Anita's colleague, Madeline Lane—the woman who'd had the audacity to throw you out of the library. You got to kill two birds with one stone. I don't imagine it was difficult for you to take Madeline's steak knife. She wouldn't have noticed because she'd finished her meal. Where did you hide after the library had closed? In one of the store cupboards? Is that where you got changed into your uniform after you'd killed Anita?"

"Jo Jo was my favourite. I'd had her since she was a pup."

"Anita didn't poison your dog."

"Of course she did."

"Look at this." I passed her the newspaper, which I'd brought from The Bugle archives. "There was a spate of dog poisonings around that time. All of them Irish setters. They caught the guy who was doing it not long after Jo Jo was killed."

Roxy began to read the article.

"I had no idea." The colour drained from her face, and she dropped the newspaper. "I swear I had no idea."

"Didn't you get a visit from a uniformed police officer?"

"No. Like I said, the police weren't interested."

"I think they will be now."

I made a call to Jack Maxwell.

***

Ever since my night out with Mad, something had been playing on my mind, and try as I might, I couldn't shake it.

On that night, I'd left the club earlier than Mad. It had been pouring with rain, and I'd been contemplating whether to go back inside, or go to the high street to try to get a taxi. When Drake had pulled up, I'd been delighted to see him, but I couldn't understand what he was doing there in the early hours of the morning. When I'd asked, he'd said he'd been at some business function or other, but what kind of business function goes on until that time in the morning? And, why was he on that particular road? The thing which was really nagging at me was that he'd taken me straight home without ever asking where I lived. As far as I could recall, I'd never told him my address.

It probably didn't mean anything. I was almost certain it was nothing, but I'm a private investigator, and I'm paid to be curious, so I decided to take a look around his flat. I wasn't exactly sure what I was looking for.

I knew that Grandma had a set of keys to his flat, which she kept in the back office of Ever. She didn't know I knew, but I don't miss a thing. Like I said, I'm a P.I.

I had to wait until Grandma wasn't around, so I asked Kathy to give me a call when she'd gone out. Of course, Kathy had wanted to know why, so I'd fed her a line about organising a surprise birthday party. On reflection, that had been a mistake because Kathy would no doubt be hankering after an invitation.

When I got Kathy's call, I hurried down there.

"When is this party?" Kathy asked as soon as she saw me.

Thank goodness for the 'forget' spell.

I hurried to the back office, grabbed the key off the hook, and made my way up the side stairs to Drake's apartment.

What exactly was I looking for? I had absolutely no idea.

As I let myself in, something Grandma had said came back to me. I'd accused her of carrying out surveillance on the flat to keep an eye on me, but she'd insisted it wasn't about me; it was about Drake. She'd asked what I knew about him. The truth was, I knew very little about him. I didn't even know what line of business he was in. Maybe, I'd be able to find something which would fill in the gaps.

I started in the bedroom, and pulled open the drawer of one of two identical bedside cabinets. It was empty. The drawer below was also empty. As were the other two. I walked around the bed, and checked the matching bedside cabinet. Again, all of the drawers were empty. I tried the wardrobe. Empty! It was the same story in the living room. Twenty minutes later, I'd covered the whole flat.

Every drawer and cupboard in the place was empty!

I couldn't get my head around what I'd found at Drake's flat. Or more accurately, what I hadn't found. It would have been nice to talk to someone about this, but who? I didn't want to mention it to my Candlefield family because it would inevitably have got back to Grandma. She had a habit of acting first, and asking questions later. I couldn't talk to my Washbridge family for obvious reasons. There was always Daze, but I'd already recruited her to follow my father who I'd suspected of being TDO. She had enough on her plate. My only option was to confront Drake myself, but that wasn't going to be easy. How would I explain why I'd been in his flat?

***

When I got back to my office, I found Winky sitting on the windowsill next to the open window. His brother's microlight was next to him. Socks was sitting on the floor looking up at Winky.

"Bro, be careful. What are you doing with my microlight?"

"Chill, bro. I just brought it up here, so I could get a better look at it. It's one mean machine."

"Sure is. I've only had it a couple of months. It's much faster than the old model."

"How much did it cost?"

"Just over four hundred pounds."

"As much as that?"

Then, without warning, Winky pushed the microlight out of the open window.

"Whoops!"

"What have you done, bro?" Socks looked horrified, and jumped onto the windowsill, next to Winky.

"Sorry, bro." Winky didn't look the slightest bit sorry.

It took all of my efforts not to burst out laughing. Socks was staring at the pavement below. I could only imagine what state his microlight was in.

"Why did you do that, bro? It's totally wrecked. I'll never be able to repair it."

"How very sad."

"I don't understand. Why?"

"There's your answer—over there!" Winky gestured across the way, where Bella was in her window. Socks knew the game was up.

"This is your fault!" He glared at me, accusingly. "You grassed me up, didn't you?"

"Never mind who told me," Winky said. "How could you do it to me, bro? How could you steal my girlfriend? Bella and I go way back."

"I didn't mean to, bro. I can't help it if I'm irresistible. You didn't have to break my microlight."

"If you don't get out of here right now, I'll break more than your microlight."

"You wouldn't hurt your own brother."

"Don't kid yourself."

Socks took one look at Winky, and knew he meant business.

"Don't expect me to come back."

"Good. Now, get gone."

Socks jumped off the windowsill, and started for the door. As he passed by me, I felt a sharp pain in my calf. He'd scratched me!

"Come here, you!" I screamed, as he bolted for the door.

I chased him through the outer office, but he was too fast for me. By the time I reached the top of the stairs, he was already out of the building.

"What's going on, Jill?" Mrs V looked puzzled. "Was that your cat?"

"No. That was another cat."

"How many have you got in there?"

"Just the one now."

Winky was on the sofa.

"Are you okay?" I asked.

"I guess so."

"What about Bella? What are you going to do about her?"

"I don't know." He shrugged. "If she wants Socks, she can have him."

"That's the spirit. There's plenty more fish in the sea."

"Talking of fish, I'm a little peckish. Red not pink, obviously."

Talk about playing the pity card.

Chapter 15

"Have you been out with Armi again, Mrs V?"

"Not since we went to his club, but he has dropped by the office a few times, and we've chatted. I hope you don't mind."

"Not at all. As long as you don't get too amorous in here."

"Jill, really!" She flashed me a look of disdain. "He's asked me to go around to his office later today. We're going to go over my Will."

The cad! It was just as I'd suspected. Armi *was* the goblin. I couldn't let him get away with this. I had to stop him before he conned Mrs V out of her life's savings.

I hurried over to Armitage, Armitage, Armitage and Poole where Jules was on reception.

"Good morning, Miss Gooder. Do you have an appointment?"

"No. Where's Joseph Armitage?"

"I'm afraid you can't see him without an appointment."

"Where's his office?"

"It's over there, but like I said, you can't see him without—"

I made a beeline straight for Armi's office, and burst through the door.

"I know your game, goblin!" I yelled at him. "Leave Mrs V alone or you'll have me to deal with!"

The small man looked terrified, and appeared to be trembling. He wasn't fooling anyone. The goblin had obviously somehow taken over Joseph Armitage's body.

"Did you hear what I said? Leave Mrs V alone, you horrible little goblin."

"Okay. Sorry." He whimpered.

As I made my way out, I caught sight of Gordon Armitage who was staring at me, open-mouthed.

He could think what he wanted. They all could. I wasn't going to stand idly by while a goblin conned my PA.

The adrenaline was still pumping as I made my way back to the office. As I turned the corner, I practically bumped into Daze and Blaze.

"Steady on, Jill. Where's the fire?"

"Sorry, Daze. How's the painting coming along?"

"Almost done."

"When you've finished that, you'd better hurry up and take that goblin into custody before he causes any more problems."

"You don't have to worry about that. We arrested him yesterday. He's behind bars in Candlefield."

Oh bum!

***

Fortunately for me, Mrs V wasn't at her desk when I got back to the office. Maybe, if I kept my head down, I'd get away with my little faux pas.

Whoops! Spoke too soon. She burst into my office.

"I've got a bone to pick with you, Jill."

"A toe bone?"

"What?" She looked understandably puzzled.

"Just my little joke."

"I'm not in the mood for your jokes. I'm very annoyed with you."

"With me?" I gave her my *butter wouldn't melt* expression. "What have I done?"

"Don't come the innocent. I'll have you know Armi is extremely upset. He told me what you did. Bursting into his office like that, and calling him a goblin."

"Did I really do that?" I shook my head. "I've been taking some new meds for my hay fever. They make me rather drowsy. I think I must have been sleepwalking."

She gave me a doubtful look.

"Please tell him I'm very sorry, and that it was all caused by my meds. Tell him I don't think he looks like a goblin. Not at all."

"Sometimes, Jill, I worry about you."

She went back to her office, and slammed the door behind her.

Winky jumped onto the desk. "What have you done to upset the old bag lady now?" He laughed.

"Nothing."

"You must have done something. Come on, you can share with me."

"I thought her new boyfriend was actually a goblin who was trying to con her out of her money."

"Wow! Those meds must really have been strong!"

***

I'd been so busy trying to clear Mad's name, that I'd allowed the Wand of Magna case to slide. But I'd just heard that Mad had been released and was on her way back home, so now I could focus my attention on the robbery at the museum.

Elizabeth Myles, the art restorer, was a quiet, timid woman who clearly loved her job.

"Have you worked here long?"

"I did my apprenticeship here underneath."

"Underneath what?"

She laughed. "Under Graham Neath. He held this job before me, and taught me practically everything I know."

"I take it Mr Neath no longer works here?"

"He's been retired for three years now. I hate to think what he'd say if he ever found out the wand had been stolen."

"Hopefully, I'll be able to get it back, so he need never know."

"I certainly hope so. Haven't I seen your picture in The Candle?"

"It's possible."

"Weren't you that woman with the world's tallest aspidistra?"

"No. That wasn't me."

"Strange. You look just like her. Do you grow aspidistras?"

"No." This interview seemed to be getting away from me.

"Did you see anything or anyone suspicious on the days leading up to the theft?"

"No, but then I'm usually locked away in my workshop. I sometimes don't see anyone except the other staff all day."

"Can you think of anyone who might have wanted to steal the wand?"

She hesitated. "I don't want to get anyone into trouble."

"Please. It's important you tell me anything you know."

"When I heard it had gone, my first thought was wow."

"Wow?"

"Wands Or War. It's a small, but vocal pressure group who believe that all witches should carry wands."

"Had they threatened to steal it?"

"No, but they've held a number of demonstrations outside the museum."

"Do you know where I can find W.O.W?"

"Sorry, no."

I thanked Elizabeth for her time. I would have to pay a visit to W.O.W — assuming I could find them.

I still hadn't managed to catch up with Sandra Bell, but I'd now explored every nook and cranny of the museum with the exception of the basement. Coral Fish had said I was welcome to go down there, but warned me that there was nothing to see.

The door to the basement was unlocked. Even with the light on, it was still quite dark as I walked down the creaky wooden steps. It wasn't at all what I'd been expecting. The museum itself was fairly large, but the basement was a single, small room with a door at the far end. Just as Coral had said, the room was completely empty. Then I remembered this had originally been the basement of Magna's house, which is why it had a much smaller footprint than the building which now stood above it.

I was fascinated by the sealed room, which I'd heard so much about. Magna Mondale herself had sealed the door with magic, and it had remained sealed ever since despite numerous efforts to open it.

Once I was sure that no one had followed me, I reached out and took hold of the door handle. I couldn't help myself—I just had to try it.

It wouldn't budge. I cast the 'power' spell, and put all of my weight behind it, but still nothing.

What else had I expected?

***

I'd hardly got through Kathy's door before both Mikey and Lizzie came rushing up to me. Their faces were beaming with excitement.

"What's going on, kids?"

"Mummy's famous," Lizzie squealed.

"Mum's a TV star," Mikey shouted.

Oh dear. Those poor deluded kids were under the impression that because their mother had been on a reality TV show for a week, she was somehow famous. It wouldn't have been so bad if it had been on network TV, but this was Wool TV. How many people watched that?

Kathy appeared.

"Come here, you two. Let Auntie Jill get in the door."

"They've just been telling me they have a famous mum."

"They're right. Would you like my autograph?"

"Come on, Kathy. It's only Wool TV."

"It may be only Wool TV to you, but do you have any idea how many people watch that station?"

"Ten?"

"Two hundred and fifty thousand."

"Never. I don't believe you."

"It's true. You can look it up. And that's just in this country. I believe it's syndicated abroad too."

"Even so, who's going to remember a silly reality TV show about a wool shop?"

"Maybe people won't remember the program, but I think they might remember me."

Wow! Just wow!

"You really have let this go to your head, haven't you?"

"I've had three hundred and sixty-five emails."

"All complaining about Everlasting Wool?"

"All wanting a signed photograph of yours truly."

I laughed. "Yeah, funny."

"Would you like to see them?"

"Are you serious?"

"Deadly. And not only that. I have over four thousand friends on my Facebook page."

"Four thousand? How many did you have before?"

"Twelve."

"Are they real people?"

"Of course they're real. They're my fans."

"Fans?"

"What else would you call them?"

"Inmates?"

"I should have known you wouldn't give me any credit, but I'll have you know that lots of people enjoyed my performance."

"Excuse me." I sniggered. "Did you just say *performance*? You weren't in a play. You were working in a wool shop."

"As I was saying, a lot of people have said my performance stole the show. They reckon I have a pleasing personality. I'm actually thinking of starting my own fan club. And, there's talk of a second series because it was so popular."

"What does Grandma think of that idea?"

"She's not so keen."

"How come?"

"It didn't turn out the way she'd hoped. She thought sales would go through the roof, but all it did was attract everyone with a grievance to come and air their complaints live on TV."

"Oh dear." I really shouldn't laugh. Snigger.

"Your grandmother had a lot of emails too."

"Really?"

"Yeah, but they all said what a horrible person she was."

"Will you take part in a second series if there is one?"

"I might unless I get a better offer."

"Better offer? From who?"

"You know how it is. Reality TV celebrities end up on all sorts of quiz programs and panel games. I might even get asked to go into the jungle."

Oh boy!

Chapter 16

I couldn't understand why I was finding it so hard to pin down Sandra Bell, so I called in on Coral Fish.

"Morning, Jill. Any progress?"

"Not a lot, to be honest. I've been trying to track down Sandra Bell for days, but I'm not having much luck."

"That's my fault. I should have mentioned that she isn't based here permanently. She's more of an independent contractor. She mainly handles P.R. in the private sector. You're in luck, though. I'm due to meet her later today. You can use my office to talk to her before we start our meeting, if you like?"

"That would be great, thanks."

As Sandra Bell wasn't due to arrive for a couple of hours, I decided to take a well-earned break at Cuppy C.

What? P.I. work can be mentally demanding. And blueberry muffins are renowned for their brain cell regeneration powers.

***

The twins were giddy with excitement. I'd completely forgotten it was the first of their craft days.

"Jill! We knew you'd want to be here for the pottery demonstration," Amber said.

"I wouldn't have missed it for the world."

They'd brought in a couple of assistants to help them cope with the extra customers they were expecting, but with fifteen minutes to go before the start, it wasn't looking very promising. There were only five customers in the whole shop, and one of them was the husband of the woman who would be doing the demonstration. Still, Amber and Pearl were still upbeat, and confident that everything would turn out well.

"We've run an ad in The Candle," Amber said. "It cost a small fortune, but it'll be worth it. We'll show Miles Best who he's dealing with."

Pearl introduced me to the woman who was sitting behind the potter's wheel. "Jill, this is Matilda, Matilda Waltz. She'll be doing the demonstration today."

"Nice to meet you, Jill." Matilda offered me her hand which was caked in clay. Yuk! "Have you ever thrown a pot, Jill?"

"I can't say I have." Unless you count those I've hurled at Winky.

"You're welcome to have a go, if you'd like to."

"Thanks, but I think I'll just watch."

When it was time for Matilda to begin, there were still only seven people in the shop, and they seemed to be regulars who were just there for a drink and a cake. No one appeared to be taking any notice of Matilda. The twins were beginning to look a little concerned.

Matilda obviously knew her stuff, but her voice was boring and monotonous. I saw a couple of people drink up and leave much quicker than they would normally have done. This wasn't good. She seemed to be driving the customers away.

After half an hour, there were only three customers left in the shop; the whole thing had clearly been a disaster. Across the road at Best Cakes, the place was absolutely packed, so I decided to check out what entertainment they had on. It was so busy over there that it was difficult to see, but I eventually caught a glimpse of the performer—it was a sword swallower. Cuppy C's pottery demonstration was never going to compete with that.

When Matilda had cleared away her stuff and left, I sat down with the twins. They were trying to remain upbeat.
"How did you think it went today?" I asked.
"A little disappointing," Amber admitted.
"Yeah, we thought we might get a few more through the door," Pearl said. "Still, the next one will be better."
"What is it next time?"
"Origami."
Oh dear.

***

"Organising P.R. for the museum can be quite challenging," Sandra Bell said. "It's a very hard sell. Unfortunately, there's nothing glamorous about a museum. Nothing exciting—certainly not for the youngsters. It's a horrible thing to say, but when I heard that the wand had gone missing, my first thought was that it would make a great story."
Sandra Bell was your typical P.R. type. Larger than life, and bubbling over with enthusiasm.
"Did you suggest that to Coral?"
"Of course, but she shot me down in flames. Coral doesn't subscribe to the idea that 'No publicity is bad publicity'. But, I'm still hoping to change her mind. That's partly what our meeting is about today. The Candle would be all over a story like this."
"Do you think Coral will let you run it?"
"Knowing her, probably not. It might help if you backed

me up."

"Me? Why would she listen to me?"

"A story in The Candle might generate some leads for you to follow up."

That was certainly true, but it would also bring out the nutjobs who always latched onto this kind of thing:

I think my pet snake has swallowed the wand. He's been all out of shape recently.

I saw the wand in my newsagent, but it was a different colour and a different shape.

I saw it in the zoo. Or maybe that was a Zebra.

"Sorry, but I don't think I should get involved. I wouldn't feel right about putting pressure on Coral to publicise the theft."

"Fair enough." She shrugged. "What do you think are the chances of finding it?"

"I honestly don't know. There's very little to go on at the moment, but I'm still hopeful."

"If you don't find it, I think this place is finished. The museum without the wand will be just an empty shell." She checked her watch. "Sorry, but I'll have to catch up with Coral now. I have another appointment straight after that one."

"Good luck trying to get her to change her mind."

"Thanks. I have a feeling I'm going to need it."

***

Wands or War? Who comes up with this rubbish?

I wanted to pay them a visit, but first I needed to find out as much about the organisation as I could. In the human world, I would have simply turned to my trusty friend,

Google, but in Candlefield there was no internet, so I had to rely on the library. I managed to dig up a little information in the archive section—The Candle had run a few articles on them. W.O.W. believed that a witch's wand was far more than just a symbol. To them, it was the very essence of witchcraft. They'd campaigned long and hard to bring back the wand, but with little success, apparently. They believed it should be mandatory for witches to carry a wand with them at all times. It was a very radical position, and one that didn't seem to have garnered much support. W.O.W. had held numerous demonstrations and sit ins—they'd even chained themselves to the Town Hall railings once. And whilst this had attracted a certain amount of publicity, it didn't appear to have translated into increased support.

I'd managed to find an address for what was apparently W.O.W's headquarters—it was very near to Beryl Christy's bakery. The name on the building was The Cheese Exchange—I had no idea why. W.O.W. had a small office on the first floor. The witch who answered the door had her hair combed in a centre parting with purple hair on one side, and green on the other. A few stray strands of green hair had drifted over to the purple side, but I didn't feel it was my place to point it out. She was wearing a conventional witch's costume—the only other time I'd seen a witch do that had been in the tournaments. There was a wand poking out from one of her pockets.

"Hi, my name's Jill Gooder. I'm a private investigator. Would it be possible to speak to whoever's in charge?"

She eyed me up and down for the longest moment. "Wait here," she said. Then she slammed the door in my face.

I was left kicking my heels for several minutes, and was

beginning to think that no one was going to talk to me. But, then the door opened again. This time, it was a tall witch with tight, curly blonde hair who came to the door. She too was dressed in full witch's outfit, and was holding a wand, which she pointed at me.

"A private investigator, you say?"

"That's right."

"What do you want with us?"

"I'd just like to ask a few questions."

"What about?"

"The Wand of Magna."

"I see. You'd better come in."

The interior of the office was very dingy, and smelled of cheese. Perhaps a legacy of the Cheese Exchange? There were another two witches inside; they too were dressed in conventional witch's outfits, and both had wands.

"My name's Desdemona." It was the tall witch with the tight, curly, blonde hair who spoke. "Come into my office; we can talk there."

I followed her through to an even smaller room which had a single light set in the ceiling. For some reason, it had been fitted with a red bulb—it was like being in a photographer's dark room.

"Sit!" Desdemona pointed to one of two plastic chairs next to a plastic table.

"Thank you. I understand your organisation has been campaigning for the return of wands."

"That's our raison d'etre, but you said you wanted to ask about the Wand of Magna."

"I assume you're familiar with it?"

"Of course I'm familiar with it. We at W.O.W. hate everything it stands for. It was Magna Mondale who was responsible for persuading witches to forsake their wands. If it wasn't for her, witches would still have them today. You're a witch. Surely you understand the importance of the wand?"

"I only recently discovered I'm a witch. I honestly haven't given much thought to the subject of wands."

"Well, it's time you did. The wand is as essential to a witch as these robes. That's what our organisation is about — returning to traditional values."

"What does the Wand of Magna represent to you?"

"It doesn't represent anything to me. It just happens to have belonged to the woman who single-handedly did more to damage witchcraft than anyone before or since."

"Okay. Let me get this straight. If the museum was to offer you the wand to use as part of your campaign, would you accept it?"

"Of course not. All that fuss over one wand is ridiculous. We want *all* witches to have wands."

"Do you have any demonstrations planned at the moment?"

"Do you seriously think I'd tell you if we did? We're a guerrilla organisation. We strike when no one expects it, in order to cause the maximum disruption."

"Of course. How many members are there in W.O.W?"

"Including those here today?"

"Yeah."

"Thirteen." She hesitated. "Well, twelve now, I suppose. Deirdre has defected."

"Deirdre?"

"Yeah. She couldn't handle the smell of cheese. Lactose intolerant, I believe."

"I see. Well, thank you very much for your time. It's been

illuminating."

Wow! Or should I say W.O.W?

I came away convinced that W.O.W. were unlikely to have been behind the theft. Not just because they appeared to have little or no interest in the wand, but also because they were quite clearly graduates from the school of nutjobs.

***

It was time to report back to Coral Fish.

"Hi, Jill. Any news?"

"Nothing so far I'm afraid. Your staff have been extremely helpful though. Elizabeth put me onto W.O.W."

"Do you think they might have stolen it?"

"I thought it was a possibility, but having spoken to their leaders, I'm not convinced they'd have the combined IQ to organise such a thing."

"Where does that leave us?"

"Sandra told me she'd like to let the press have the story. That might help."

"No! I've already told her that's a non-starter."

"Fair enough. I had thought I might find some clues somewhere in the museum, but I've covered it from top to bottom, except the sealed room of course. No joy so far, I'm afraid."

"Do you have any theories, at least?"

"The fact that you haven't received a demand of any kind suggests to me that the wand may have ended up in the hands of a collector."

Coral nodded. "That's precisely what I think. In some ways I hope it has because then at least that would mean the wand will be safe."

"I haven't given up on this case yet. I'm going to try to track down some of the collectors to see if I turn anything up."

"Thanks, Jill. I really appreciate your help."

Chapter 17

I'd been asked to meet the captains of the three men's BoundBall teams: Wayne Holloway, the werewolves' captain, Aaron Benway, the wizards' captain, and Archie Maine, the vampires' captain. I was headed for the BoundBall clubhouse, which is where I'd first met them some time ago when I'd been asked to investigate the disappearance of the Candlefield Cup. In fact, I'd discovered that the cup was never *actually* missing, but the incident had led to the resolution of a long-running feud between the wizard team and the other two teams.

"Hello again, gentlemen."

The three of them greeted me with smiles and handshakes.

"Have a seat, Jill," Archie said. "It's really good to see you again."

"I see the cup's still here, then?"

"Yes. There haven't been any more disappearing acts I'm pleased to say. How's the P.I. business going?"

"Slow, probably best describes it."

"You've no doubt already guessed why we wanted to speak with you?"

"Could it possibly be about a certain fundraising event in aid of SupAid?"

"The three of us have been discussing this," Aaron said. "And we're really not sure it's a good idea."

"Rubbish!"

They all seemed taken aback by my blunt response. They'd obviously forgotten how tactful and reserved I could be.

"Surely you should have learned from the mistakes of the

past," I said. "Exclusion is never a good thing. It doesn't matter if it's exclusion based on sup type, as happened to the wizards, or exclusion based on gender."

"But women have never played BoundBall," Wayne said.

"That's where you're wrong. Women most certainly *do* play BoundBall. Not in the same numbers as men, granted. The problem is their sport gets no coverage whatsoever. They're ignored by the press, or worse still, treated as a joke."

"I'm sure that isn't true," Wayne said.

"I can assure you it is. You only have to look at the article The Candle ran on this event. You'd be hard pressed to find a more patronising and condescending piece of sports journalism. Anyway, what harm can it possibly do? Surely it's all about the game, regardless of gender?"

"I'm not even sure you'll be able to put a team together in time," Aaron said.

"That comment just underlines what I've already said. Our problem isn't finding enough players—we already have far more than we need. It's having to disappoint those who don't make the cut."

"Do you intend to play yourself, Jill?" Wayne asked.

"Me? No. I've never played the game, but I have agreed to act as team manager. I've already appointed a captain who will handle team selection."

"You seem pretty determined to go ahead with this."

"Oh, it's going to happen. Trust me on that one. But, I'm sure the game would be even more successful if you three gentlemen are willing to endorse it."

They looked at one another as though uncertain what to say or do. Eventually, it was Archie who spoke. "Would you mind giving us a few minutes, Jill?"

"Certainly." I stepped out of the clubhouse and waited outside. Five minutes later, Archie called me back in.

"Look, Jill, I'll be completely honest with you. We still have our reservations, but we owe you a great deal for the help you gave us."

"Does that mean you'll officially endorse the event?"

"We'll be happy to."

"Thank you, gentlemen. And, I trust you'll all be there on the day?"

"We wouldn't miss it for the world. This is the biggest thing to happen to BoundBall for many a year."

No pressure then.

***

While I was in Candlefield, I called in to check on Barry.

"I want to go for a walk. Can I go for a walk? Please, Jill, can I go for a walk?"

"Yes, okay, we'll go to the park."

"Can we go and get Babs? Can we? Can we go get Babs?"

"I'll give Dolly a ring now and see if she's in."

"Babs is my girlfriend."

"Yeah. I'm not sure about that. Has she actually said she is?"

"She doesn't need to—I can tell."

"Okay, well, I'd better give Dolly a ring first to make sure it's okay."

I tried Dolly's number, but there was no reply, so I gave her daughter, Dorothy, a call.

"I just rang your mother. I was hoping to take Babs for a walk, but she's not answering her phone."

"She's gone away on an artist's retreat for the weekend,

and she's taken Babs with her."

"An *artist's* retreat?"

"Don't laugh."

"I wouldn't dream of it. Incidentally, did you know your mum had done a portrait of my sister and her family?"

"Oh dear. How did that work out? As if I didn't know."

"I haven't seen the end result yet."

"How did your sister take it?"

"She's still in a state of shock, I think."

"I'm really sorry."

"No need for you to apologise. I'm sure Kathy will soon get over it now she's a TV celebrity."

"TV celebrity?"

"Do you watch Wool TV?"

"Is there such a thing?"

"That is the correct answer. I'll explain the next time I see you. I'd better be going because Barry is getting impatient."

"You're out of luck, Barry. Babs has gone away for the weekend."

"Why didn't she ask me to go with her?"

"I don't think they had any spare tickets."

"Can we go to the park, anyway? I like the park. I want to go for a walk."

"Why not?"

As soon as I'd let Barry off his lead, he began to run around the park, but I'd learned my lesson, so instead of chasing after him, I found a bench, sat down and waited. He'd eventually run out of steam, and come to find me.

I'd been there for about thirty minutes when I spotted Drake in the distance. He was making his way towards the gate at the bottom end of the park. This was my opportunity to have it out with him. But how? I wasn't sure of the best way to tackle it.

"Drake!" I chased down the path after him, even though I still had no idea what I was going to say.

He turned around. "Hi, Jill. Is Barry with you?"

"Yeah, he's around somewhere. Look, I'd like a word, if you've got a minute."

"Of course."

"I'll get straight to the point."

"You're making this sound very serious."

"There's no easy way to say this, so I'll just come right out with it."

Oh boy! I wished I'd thought it through first.

"The other day, I let myself into your flat."

"What?"

"I'm sorry. I know I shouldn't have, but the point is—what I wanted to say—I mean." This was going well. "Why are all the drawers empty? You have nothing in that flat at all."

"Oh, that? Right."

"So?"

"I *was* going to tell you, but I didn't know how to."

"Tell me what?"

"I've given up the flat."

"But you've barely had time to get settled in. Why?"

"Your grandmother told me that you were seeing someone. A policeman, she said."

"Grandma told you that?"

"Yes. She seemed to take great delight in doing so."

"I still don't understand why you gave up the flat? I thought you wanted it for when you're in Washbridge on business?"

"Not really. I know that's what I said, but the truth is I'd hoped that if I had a base in Washbridge, maybe you and I would become closer. So, when I found out that you were with someone, I couldn't see the point in keeping it on. I moved out a few days ago."

"I see. I'm sorry, I didn't realise."

"That's okay. Win some, lose some. Look, I can't hang around. There's somewhere I need to be."

"Okay. See you around then, I guess."

And with that, he was gone. No wonder there was nothing in the flat. I'd had no idea that the only reason he took it on was in the hope that he and I might become closer.

I felt awful.

***

Back at Cuppy C, I was giving Barry some Barkies when Hamlet called to me. I'd been giving him a wide berth because that hamster had a bad habit of spending my money — money I didn't have.

"Hi, Hamlet. How are you?"

"Very well, thank you, Jill."

"Are you out of books again?"

"No. We seem to have overcome that little problem. One of our reading club members lives quite close to the library, so he's able to bring a new supply of books with him to every meeting."

"That's great."

"I do, however, have another slight problem."

"What's that?"

"Between you and me, I'm worried that I'm getting a little out of shape."

He flexed his arms and touched his tummy.

"You look okay to me."

"It's kind of you to say that, but I'm afraid it isn't true. I need to exercise more."

"But surely you have your wheel?"

"Yes, but that's only good for cardiovascular exercise. I don't have any problems in that area; I can run for miles and miles. It's my body shape I'm worried about. I'm losing definition—even becoming a little flabby in some areas."

"What do you want to do about it?"

"I'm going to need some equipment. I thought maybe some dumbbells would do the trick. Nothing too expensive."

"I assume that would be rodent edition dumbbells?"

"Of course. I don't think I could manage the human variety." He laughed.

"No, quite."

"I wondered if you could see your way clear to getting some for me? I'd be most grateful."

"I wish I could, but I haven't had much work recently, and my finances are stretched to the limit as it is."

"I wouldn't expect you to pay; I just need you to collect them. I'll give you my credit card and the pin number."

Now, I was confused.

"But, as I understood it, there are no credit cards or debit cards, or plastic of any kind in Candlefield."

"That's right—at least for sups. They can't be trusted with them. But there are credit cards available for rodents. It's the RodentCash system."

"O—kay." I should have known.

***

Bill Ratman was behind the counter in Everything Rodent. "Have you come back for an e-reader?"

"No. I'm on a different mission today. Hamlet, that's my hamster, is a bit concerned that he's out of shape. He's lost definition, apparently."

"A common problem," Bill said. "Most of the hamsters have superb cardiovascular systems because of their wheels, but keeping in shape otherwise can be very difficult for them. Let me guess, he sent you here to look for some equipment to get him back in shape?"

"That's right. He's asked me to look at dumbbells."

"Dumbbells? You can do much better than that. What about a cross-trainer? He could exercise so many different muscle groups with one of those."

"No, I think I'll just stick with the dumbbells."

"Actually, I also run another business—a sort of sister company which is only a couple of streets away. It's called Rodent Fitness. You may have noticed it?"

"I can't say I have."

"I could do a very good deal on twelve months' membership for your hamster. We have all the latest equipment in there: treadmills, cross trainers, rowing machines, you name it."

"Thanks, but I think I'll stick to the dumbbells."

"Okay, sure. They're over there to the left."

I made my way over to the rodent exercise equipment. There was everything you could need for a rodent home gym: dumbbells, barbells, and all manner of equipment for bodybuilding and weightlifting.

"Are you sure the prices on these are correct?"

"Oh yes."

"But they're so small."

"But all precision-made."

I picked up a couple of dumbbells and took them over to the counter. They weighed next to nothing, but I guessed for a hamster they would be quite heavy.

"That'll be seventy-six pounds, please."

I was clearly in the wrong business!

I passed Hamlet's tiny credit card to Bill who put it into a small handheld machine with the word 'RodentCash' on it. At first, I struggled to type in the pin because the keys were so small. In the end, I had to get a pen out of my bag, and use the tip to press the keys.

Back at the flat, I put the dumbbells in Hamlet's cage.

"Excellent, Jill. Thank you very much."

"Here's your card back."

"Thank you."

"The owner of Everything Rodent tried to sell me a cross-trainer."

"That would be a sledgehammer to crack a nut. These are all I need."

"He also has a fitness club. He tried to sell me a membership for you."

"I'm not surprised. He's into everything, that fellow. Anyway, thank you for these."

I turned to leave.

"Oh, and by the way, Jill—"

"Yes?"

"Have you considered investing in some exercise equipment? A bit of toning up wouldn't do *you* any

harm."
Cheek!

Chapter 18

"But I hate picnics." I groaned.

Kathy gave me her patented, *'Jill's being a pain again'* look.

"Jill, would you mind doing me a tiny favour, please?"

"What now?"

"Stop your moaning."

"But picnics are so naff. Wasp sandwiches? Yuk! And, it's muddy and there are smelly cows everywhere."

"What you've just described there? It's called the countryside. *Everyone* loves the countryside."

"Not me. Can't we have the picnic in the town centre instead?"

She rolled her eyes. "You, me, Lizzie and Mikey are going into the countryside. We're going to have sandwiches, cakes, and pop. And, we're all going to enjoy ourselves. That's an order!"

"What about Peter? How come he gets let off the hook?"

"Pete's working. He's busy."

"I'm busy."

"You told me yesterday that you didn't have any work on."

"Yeah, but a case came in late last night."

"What case was that?"

"It was — err — a missing — err — armadillo."

"Armadillo?"

"Yeah. It belongs to an eccentric millionaire. He collects them, and one of them is missing." I noticed the look on her face. "You don't believe me, do you?"

"No, Jill, I don't believe you. Armadillo? Is that the best you could come up with? Even by your standards, that's pretty bad."

She was right. If I'd had more warning, I could have come up with a much better excuse. Missing armadillo? What was I thinking? I deserved to go on the picnic.

"Look, Auntie Jill! Zebodile is coming on the picnic with us." Lizzie held up the monstrous beanie for me to see.

"That's great."

"And I'm bringing my drum." Mikey started hitting it for all he was worth.

"Fantastic!"

It just got better and better.

It was only ten miles to the picnic site, but it felt like a thousand. I was in the back seat sandwiched between Lizzie, who kept showing me her horrific beanie, and Mikey, who was playing his drum. And, I use the term 'playing' very loosely.

"Why can't I sit up front with you, Kathy?" I shouted over the noise of the drum.

"There's no room."

"Couldn't you put the hamper in the boot?"

"It's full. Pete's tools are in there."

"Why can't the hamper go in the back with the kids instead of up front with you?"

"Because the kids would eat all of the buns before we even get there."

"Would you like to hold Zebodile, Auntie Jill?"

"Listen to me play my favourite tune, Auntie Jill."

By the time we arrived at the picnic site, I'd almost lost the will to live.

"Come and throw the Frisbee, Auntie Jill." Mikey had at last put the drum down.

"I'm not really very good with Frisbees."

"It's easy, Auntie Jill." Lizzie grabbed my hand.

"Look!" Mikey threw the Frisbee towards Lizzie. She tried to catch it, but it went sailing over her head.

"That was too high, Mikey," she complained.

"No it wasn't. You're just rubbish at catching."

"Kids," Kathy warned them. "No arguing or we go home."

Lizzie went chasing after the Frisbee, grabbed it, and threw it in my direction. It was too high, and even though I jumped, I still missed it, so I had to go chasing after the stupid thing. Have I mentioned I hated Frisbees?

Before I could pick it up, a dog appeared from nowhere, grabbed it in its mouth, and went dashing off into the distance. Oh dear. How very sad. No more Frisbee. Snigger.

"Sorry, kids. That dog's taken the Frisbee."

"Aw." Lizzie pouted. "Daddy only bought it yesterday."

"Oh well." I feigned disappointment. "Let's go and have some sandwiches."

"Where's your Frisbee?" Kathy asked the kids.

"A dog stole it," Mikey said.

"He ran off with it in his mouth." Lizzie stamped her foot in anger.

"Why didn't you get it back?" Kathy was looking at me.

"He was too fast." I shrugged. "And besides, he looked really fierce."

"Help! Somebody help me, please!" shouted a woman, about Kathy's age. She looked panic-stricken. Both Kathy and I hurried over to her.

"What's wrong?" I said.

"It's Jimmy. He's stuck. He's going to fall."

I followed her gaze, and saw a young boy hanging from a

branch high in a tree. It appeared that the only thing stopping him from falling was the belt on his trousers which had snagged on the branch.

"I didn't even realise he'd climbed the tree. I only took my eyes off him for a couple of minutes."

"It's going to be okay," Kathy reassured her.

I wasn't so sure.

"How?" The woman sounded even more desperate. "That branch won't hold his weight for long."

She was right. The branch that he was hanging from wasn't very thick. If it gave way under his weight, he'd plummet straight to the ground. If that happened, he was sure to sustain a serious injury — or worse.

"Have you called the fire brigade?" Kathy said.

"No, I didn't know what to do." The woman was becoming increasingly distraught.

"I'll do it." Kathy took out her phone and dialled nine, nine, nine. "We're at Sunset Picnic Park. There's a young boy hanging from a tree. Please hurry. He's going to fall any minute."

She'd no sooner said the words than the branch snapped, and the boy plunged towards the ground.

My instincts took over as I cast the 'faster' and 'power' spells. I reached the tree just in time to catch him.

"My name's Jimmy." He seemed totally unfazed by his brush with death.

"Are you okay?"

"Yeah. I was climbing the tree, but I slipped."

I put him down, and he seemed none the worse for his adventure.

Kathy and the boy's mother came running over. His mother scooped him up in her arms, and kissed him.

Tears were running down her cheeks.

"Thank you so much. Thank you."

Kathy still had the phone in her hand. "No, it's okay. He's down from the tree now. Yes, he's fine."

After the woman and the boy had left. Kathy stared at me. "What happened just then, Jill?"

"How do you mean?"

"One minute you were standing next to us. The next, you were at the tree — catching the boy. How did you get there so quickly?"

"I always was good in the sprint."

"But how did you catch him from that height? I'm surprised he didn't drill you into the ground."

"He wasn't *that* heavy. He's only a small boy."

Fortunately, before Kathy could press me further, two elderly women approached us.

"It's her. I told you it was her." The one with the purple rinse pointed to Kathy.

"You're right, it is."

"Can I have your autograph?" Purple Rinse rummaged through her handbag.

"You! Young lady!" The other old girl shouted to me. "Will you take my photo with Kathy."

Kathy posed for photos, and signed autographs for them both. I felt like a spare wheel.

"Does that happen often?"

"You'd be surprised, but then I guess it's the price of fame."

On the drive home, I was allowed to sit up front with Kathy. The empty picnic hamper was in the back with the kids, who were both fast asleep.

"I still don't understand what happened back there," Kathy said.

"Jimmy's okay. That's the main thing."

"I suppose so, but there's something strange going on. I've said it before. Something's different about you, and I don't know what it is."

"Maybe it's because I'm with Jack."

"Hmm?" She looked doubtful.

The journey home was through the countryside. There were very few houses, and the roads were mostly deserted. About half-way home, we drove past a lay-by. Parked in it was none other than my new friend, Malcolm, the mobile barber—as usual, he seemed to be doing a roaring trade.

***

When I got back to my flat, a note had been pushed under the door. I didn't recognise the handwriting. It said:

'I know the whereabouts of the wand. Meet me in the basement of the museum tonight at midnight.'

Who could have written it? More importantly, how had they known where I lived? And why deliver it to my flat in Washbridge rather than to the flat above Cuppy C? If the note had come from the thief, why ask to meet in the museum? Surely, they must know that was risky. They could have requested to meet anywhere—somewhere they'd know if I'd been followed—somewhere they could make a quick getaway. By meeting in the basement of the museum, they'd be effectively trapping themselves.

Or was the trap meant for me?

Even if it was, I had no choice. I had to go, but I'd need to be on my guard. This could be TDO.

**

When I arrived at the museum, the door to the main entrance was unlocked. I stepped inside, and pushed it closed behind me. There was no sign of Bert, the security guard, so I made my way to the basement. I switched the light on, and walked slowly down the steps. There was no one in there.

I paced up and down nervously as the minutes ticked by. Each one seemed to last an hour. By fifteen minutes after midnight, there was still no sign of anyone. Maybe it had all been a hoax. I was just about to go back upstairs when I heard a voice. It seemed to come from inside the sealed room. It was a voice I recognised.

"Amber?"

"Is anyone out there?" She sounded scared. "Help us, please."

And then I heard Pearl's voice. "Can anyone hear us? Please help us."

I put my ear against the door.

"Amber? Pearl? Are you in there?"

"Is anyone out there? Help us, please!"

They obviously couldn't hear me. How had they got in there, and who had locked them in?

"Please help us!" Pearl sounded desperate.

I had to do something.

"Stand back girls." I wasn't sure why I'd said that because they obviously couldn't hear me.

I cast the 'power' spell, and pushed against the door with

all of my strength.

Nothing happened.

I fired a thunder bolt at the door handle.

Still, nothing happened.

"Help us, please!" Pearl shouted.

I had to get inside, but conventional spells weren't going to work. I had to pit the strength of my mind against the magic that was keeping the door sealed.

I gripped the pendant, which I always wore around my neck. With my eyes closed, I focused all my thoughts and energy on the door. The pressure building inside my head was almost unbearable — it felt as though the top of my skull would explode at any moment.

The creaking sound brought me back to earth. I opened my eyes to find the door was ajar. Nervously, I pushed it open and stepped inside. There was a single piece of furniture: a table covered with dust. On it was an equally dusty book. I picked it up, and was about to flick through the pages when I heard a familiar voice.

"I believe you're looking for this?"

"Grandma? What are you doing here?"

She handed me something. "Is this what I think it is?"

"I expect so."

"The Wand of Magna?"

"Yes. You can return it in the morning."

"I don't understand?"

"I brought you here because I needed you to get inside this room."

"How did you know I could?"

"I wasn't sure, but I thought if you had the right motivation, you'd have the best chance of succeeding."

"I heard the twins in here." I glanced around. "Where are

they?"

"They were never in here. The voices you heard came from me. One of my better party tricks."

"So you took the wand? Just to get me in here?"

"Yes. It was ridiculously easy too. I just had to put the security guard to sleep for a few hours."

"But I still don't understand why."

"For that." She pointed to the dusty book.

"Is that Magna's spell book?"

"Take a look."

"No!" I backed away from the table. "I can't."

"Of course you can."

"No. You open it."

She sighed—clearly annoyed.

As she reached out to open it, something happened. It was as if she'd received an electric shock.

"What happened? Are you okay?"

"I'm fine. But the book clearly isn't meant for me. You open it."

"No!" I wasn't in any hurry to get a shock.

"Do it!"

It was a toss-up which I was more scared of: getting a shock from the book or getting a tongue-lashing from Grandma. Who was I kidding? I was much more scared of Grandma.

I closed my eyes, and reached for the book.

Nothing happened. No shock—nothing, so I opened my eyes.

"Just as I suspected." Grandma nodded. "The book has been waiting for you."

"I don't understand."

"You will. For now, just take it home with you. Keep it

safe, and study it as if your life depended on it."

"Will you help me?"

"I can't help you now. The book will tell you everything you need to know. Now go! And don't forget to return the wand tomorrow."

"Won't they wonder how someone got into the sealed room?"

"They won't know anyone has been in here. You're going to seal it on the way out."

"What good will that do? I don't have Magna's power."

"We'll see."

Chapter 19

It was the early hours of the morning when I eventually got back to my flat. I was drained—both mentally and physically. All I really wanted to do was go to bed and sleep forever, but I couldn't. I had Magna's book with me, and as tired as I was, I would never have been able to sleep if I didn't at least take a look at it first.

I'd managed to get a lot of the dust off, but when I dropped it onto the coffee table, a small cloud still flew up into my face, and made me sneeze. Seeing the book there took me back to when I'd first discovered I was a witch. Even though I was tired, I couldn't help but smile at the memory of my first book of spells. I'd been so confused when I received it—I'd thought it was some kind of joke. I'd even tried to throw it away, but it had come back like a bad penny. All of that seemed such a long time ago now. I hadn't believed in magic back then, but I was a very different person now.

In front of me was a book which had once belonged to the most powerful witch there had ever been. Nervously, I opened the cover; the first couple of pages were blank. Then came a page which had been handwritten:

To whoever reads this,

When I sealed this book inside my basement, I hoped that one day, a witch as powerful as I once was, would retrieve it.
I'm sure you already know the reason I sealed this book away. I feared that if it fell into the wrong hands, it could be the end of Candlefield, and maybe even the end of witchcraft. I could not take that chance.

Please take the time to read everything in this book. Use what you learn for good, and to rid Candlefield of all those who threaten to undermine its future.

Yours in witchcraft,
Magna Mondale.

I didn't know what to think. Was I really the right person to be reading this? It felt like some kind of ridiculous mistake. I'd only known I was a witch for such a short period of time, and I was still only on level three. There were so many witches who were way more powerful than I was—level six witches like Grandma. They were the ones who should have been reading the book. But then, I had managed to open the sealed door when so many others had tried and failed. Maybe, this really was my destiny.

***

The next morning, my mind was well and truly blown.
I'd only managed to read just over half of Magna's book before I'd had to admit defeat and go to bed. The contents were not at all what I'd expected. She'd come up with a new and unique way to perform magic. Using her methods, it was possible to cast existing spells much more quickly, and with so much more power. But the real revelation was how she'd found a way to combine spells. I'd used more than one spell at the same time before, but her method allowed two or more spells to be 'mixed' to form a 'brand new' spell. The possibilities were endless. The caveat was that it was incredibly difficult. I'd failed miserably in my first few attempts, but I'd slowly begun

to get the hang of it. It required more focus and energy than I'd ever had to use before. But the end results were more than worth it.

I dearly wanted to pick up where I'd left off the previous night, but it was the day of the BoundBall match, and before that, I'd arranged to meet with Daze at Cuppy C. She was going to give me an update on my father, who she'd been following at my request.

"I've been tailing him for a few days now, and he's definitely up to something. I just don't know what."

"How do you mean?"

"Just that he's been behaving very strangely. Did you know he's living in a flat above the Thimble shop in the market square?"

"There's a thimble shop?"

"Haven't you seen it? It's called 'The Finger'."

"Can't say I have. Anyway, carry on."

"He leaves his flat at the same time every day; ten o'clock on the dot. Then he walks the same route."

"Where does he go?"

"That's just it. He doesn't actually *go* anywhere. He walks a circular route which eventually brings him back to his flat."

"Perhaps he just needs the exercise? That's not so unusual is it?"

"No. Except for the days when he disappears."

"How do you mean?"

"It happens in exactly the same place each time. There's a building just beyond the market square called The Central."

"I've never heard of it."

"You wouldn't have. It's derelict now, but in its heyday, it was a popular meeting hall for any number of sup events."

"How often has this happened?"

"Twice. And both times, he was close to The Central."

"Could he have used magic to become invisible?"

"No. I would have been able to detect that. I thought perhaps there was a secret entrance, but I examined every square inch of the exterior, and I couldn't find anything. One minute he was there, and the next he was gone."

"But you say that only happened on two days?"

"That's right. The other days he just walked straight by."

"Have you seen him talking to anyone suspicious?"

"No one. Whenever I've seen him, he's been by himself."

"On the two days he disappeared, did you hang around to see what happened?"

"Yes, I waited for a couple of hours both times, but he never reappeared. And yet the next day, he was back at his flat again."

"What do you think all this means, Daze?"

"I have absolutely no idea. It's all very weird."

"Will you continue to keep tabs on him for a little longer?"

"I can manage a couple more days, but no more than that because I've got other cases stacking up. Since the other Rogue Retrievers left, it's been pretty hectic."

"I'm sorry to have to ask you."

"It's okay. I'm happy to help if I can, but I'm not convinced it's doing any good. Anyway, I'll stick with him for the next two days, and see if anything else happens. If it does I'll let you know."

"Thanks, Daze. In the meantime, I think I should take a

look at The Central."

***

Annie and Beryl Christy met us at Aunt Lucy's. Annie was so excited.

"Jill, this was a brilliant idea of yours. It's the single most successful fundraising event we've ever had. Pre-match ticket sales are off the scale. I can't thank you enough; this is going to make all the difference to SupAid."

"I'm really pleased it's raised so much money, but I must admit, I'm worried about the event itself. I'd hate for it to be a let-down after so many people have supported it."

"It won't be a let-down."

"But the women's team have an almost impossible task."

"The impossible task was setting up the game in the first place. You've already done that. The result doesn't matter."

"It matters to me, and it matters to the team too."

The twins were also at Aunt Lucy's, but there was no sign of Grandma.

"How are Alan and William taking all this?" I asked.

"They're not happy," Amber said. "Not because the match is happening, but because they're both on the bench."

"Yeah," Pearl said. "Alan's in a foul mood. But what did he expect? They've combined three teams: the wizards, the werewolves and the vampires. They can't all play. Anyway, it's not like they've been dropped altogether. They're on the bench, so they might get to play at some point."

"They've both been walking around with long faces all

week," Amber said. "And they've done nothing but talk about how many points the women's team are going to lose by."

"Who are you two supporting, anyway?"

The twins looked at me as though I'd grown another head.

"Who do you think? The women of course. Go W!"

When we arrived at the stadium, it was absolutely buzzing. There were people everywhere. Some were buying souvenirs; others were queuing to get in. Some looked as though they'd turned up just to savour the atmosphere of this unique event. It was every bit as busy as when I'd been at the BoundBall tournament, but there seemed to be far more women in the crowd today.

I'd been invited to the VIP area, but I'd declined because, as manager, I wanted to be on the bench right next to the action. Before the game started, I made my way to the changing room. As soon as I stepped inside, I could sense the nervous tension in the air.

Anthea Close climbed onto one of the benches, and delivered a rousing speech. When she finished, everyone cheered. Then she turned to me.

"Jill, will you say a few words?"

"You've already said everything there is to say, Anthea. Just go out there and do yourselves proud. Go 'W'!"

Everyone cheered!

When the match kicked off, the crowd in the stadium erupted. Even though I was team manager, and sitting on the bench, I still had no more idea about the rules of BoundBall than I'd had at the previous match. It made no sense to me whatsoever.

As the game progressed, things went from bad to worse for our team. For the first thirty minutes, it was one-way traffic as the men pounded the women's goal. They had soon pulled back thirty-five points.

Then, suddenly, our team captain broke away.

"Go on! Go on! Yes!"

She scored, and the stadium erupted. The men on the pitch looked shell-shocked.

After that, the game was a little less one-sided. By halftime, the women had managed to put eight points on the scoreboard, which gave them a total of a hundred and eight. The men were on sixty-three. In the dressing room some of the women looked dispirited. I felt like it was my responsibility to raise their morale.

"Forget the score. It doesn't matter. You have already won. After today, they'll have no choice but to recognise that women's BoundBall is here to stay. Go back out there, and enjoy yourselves. On three. One, two, three."

"Go W!"

And they *did* enjoy themselves. They gave everything they had. With only seconds remaining in the game, the scores were tied. The women's team looked absolutely exhausted. Suddenly, one of the men broke away and scored. Moments later, the final whistle blew.

The men had won by one hundred and twenty-two points to the women's one hundred and twenty-one. All of the women looked downhearted; I could have cried for them — they'd given everything and more.

But then a strange thing happened. The men formed a guard of honour next to the tunnel to the changing rooms, and applauded the women's team off the pitch.

Women's BoundBall was now well and truly on the map.

***

When I was leaving the stadium, Grandma suddenly appeared.

"I didn't think you were coming to the match, Grandma?"

"Match? What match?"

"The BoundBall. Men versus women."

"Why would I want to see that?"

"Wouldn't you like to know how the women's team got on?"

"Do I look like I care?"

She didn't.

"Why *are* you here, then?"

"Lucy tells me that Horace came to see you."

I was surprised that Aunt Lucy had mentioned it to her.

"Yes, he did. He came to my flat."

"What did he want?"

"I honestly don't know. He mentioned Kathy, Peter and the kids. Why don't you ask him yourself?"

"Horace and I have gone our separate ways."

"I'm sorry. I didn't realise. Didn't things work out?"

"Horace isn't the man I used to know. Now listen. This is very important. Do you remember anything specific he said to you while he was at your flat?"

"Only that he didn't know why I was wasting my time with humans." I hesitated.

"Go on."

"I wouldn't have said this while you two were still seeing each other, but — "

"Spit it out, woman!"

"Horace kind of gave me the creeps. It was weird—him just turning up like that. I didn't even realise he knew where I lived."

"Listen to me carefully, Jill. You must contact me immediately if he approaches you again. Do you understand?"

"Of course, but why? What's wrong, Grandma?"

"Nothing for you to worry about."

"I wasn't—until you said that."

"Everything will be fine. Look, I have to get back to Ever."

Nothing for you to worry about?

Not very reassuring. What had gone wrong between them? She'd seemed so happy that Horace was back in her life, so why had it ended so suddenly?

What exactly was going on with Horace?

Chapter 20

The next morning, I was still buzzing from the BoundBall match.

"You look very pleased with yourself, Jill." Mrs V was sorting through a pile of scarves. "What are you so happy about?"

"BoundBall."

Whoops!

"What's bound ball?"

What was I thinking? I'd been so carried away that I'd forgotten I was back in the human world.

"No, I didn't say bound ball, I said—err—round ball. I went to a round ball match."

"What's round ball?"

"You know—soccer."

"I've never heard it called round ball before. I didn't know you liked soccer."

"Oh yeah. I love it. All that offside and stuff. It's great."

"What exactly is offside? I've never really understood it."

"It's really very complicated. Oh wait. Was that my phone ringing?"

"I didn't hear anything."

"I'm sure it was my phone. I'd better go and check."

Phew! I'd really let my guard down, but I'd just about got away with it.

There was a sudden chill in the office accompanied by the sound of giggling. That could only mean one thing: The colonel and Priscilla were paying a visit. I hadn't seen them for a while, and had been wondering if they'd given any more thought to returning to the colonel's house.

When they appeared, I had my answer, and had to shield my eyes.

"Hi, Jill," the colonel said. "Are you okay? Do you have something in your eye?"

"No. I don't. You two do realise you're naked, don't you?"

"Whoops! Sorry, Jill." The colonel laughed.

Priscilla giggled. "Oh, Briggsy, aren't we silly?"

"I'm so sorry, Jill," the colonel said. "Really, this is most embarrassing. Would you prefer it if we left?"

"No, it's okay, but if you don't mind, I'll keep my hand in front of my eyes."

"Yes, of course. I'm so terribly sorry."

"I take it that you decided to go back to the house, then?"

"Yes, we did. Cilla and I talked about it for ages. We weren't sure what to do, but in the end we decided we should at least check the old place out. We thought maybe there'd be some rooms where we wouldn't come into contact with the guests."

"Hmm? I'm guessing that's not quite how things worked out."

"What gave it away?" The colonel grinned. "You're quite right. Although we did our best to avoid the new owner and his guests, it was practically impossible. They were everywhere. Wherever we went, there were naked people. The strange thing is though, although neither of us has ever considered naturism before, the more time we spent there amongst these people, the more natural it seemed. One evening, Cilla and I were enjoying a glass of elderberry wine when she asked what I thought about us going naked."

For a moment I forgot myself, and dropped my hand from my eyes. Priscilla was blushing—all over! I quickly put my hand back.

"I have to say, Priscilla, I'm a little surprised."

"Me too, Jill. If anyone had told me that I would get into naturism, I would have laughed in their face. But the truth is I feel completely liberated. Both Briggsy and I are really into it."

"So it would seem."

"I can only apologise again, Jill," the colonel said. "We wanted to tell you that we'd moved back to the house, but we've spent so much time naked recently, that it never occurred to us that we probably ought to pop some clothes on first."

"Yeah, well, if you don't mind, perhaps next time you come over—"

"Of course. We won't make a habit of this."

"What do you make of the new owner?"

"He's quite a charming chap, and he's definitely into the paranormal. Most nights, he wanders the house, and is obviously looking for us. At first, we found it quite amusing, but to be honest, the novelty has worn off now. We tend to stick to the areas of the house where he isn't likely to show up. Anyway, we won't keep you any longer. We'd better be getting back. Thanks again for checking out the house. Next time we come around, I promise we'll be fully clothed."

After they'd left, Winky said, "Are you running some kind of porn empire, now?"

"No! They're just friends."

"Naked friends?"

"They hadn't realised they were naked."

"An easy mistake to make."

I needed to get out of the office for a while, so I thought I'd pay a visit to Coffee Triangle, but when I got there I realised it was gong day. Just my luck—I hated the sound of gongs. I was just about to turn tail when I spotted two familiar faces inside. Jack was with none other than my bestie, Miles Best. They were laughing and joking, and clearly having a whale of a time. What on earth was going on?

I needed to find out what was happening, but I had to do it without letting either of them see me. After sneaking in, all secret-agent like, I found a seat on the opposite side of the shop. I didn't bother with a muffin; I was too angry to eat. It was incredibly noisy. The stupid man at the table opposite seemed to think that his gong was a drum; he was beating it ten to the dozen. Jack and Miles Best were still laughing and chatting away. How did Jack Maxwell even know Miles Best?

After about thirty minutes, Miles stood up and left, so I made my way over to Jack's table.

"Jill? I didn't know you were in here."

"I bet you didn't!" I took a seat opposite him. "What were you doing with Miles Best?"

"Whoa, steady on. Who trod on your corns?"

"Why were you with him, Jack?"

"He contacted me, and said he wanted to introduce himself as he was just opening a new P.I. business in the town."

"And what? You said, *'Yeah, okay. Let's get a coffee'*? I seem to remember when you first arrived here, you wouldn't give *me* the time of day."

"I'm trying to learn from past mistakes, and besides he emphasised that he wanted to work *with* me and not *against* me. To be fair, he seems very professional."

"Oh? And I'm not?"

"I didn't say that, Jill. Anyway, I only saw him in the first place because he said he was a friend of yours."

"A *friend of mine*?"

"Yes. Why? Isn't he?"

"Not exactly, no."

I was going to kill Miles Best.

***

I must have walked past the building known as The Central on numerous occasions, but I'd never really noticed it before. Its façade was overgrown, and the building was practically derelict. According to Daze, this was where my father had disappeared on two occasions. She'd been adamant that he hadn't made himself invisible because she would have been able to detect that. So, if he hadn't made himself invisible, where had he gone and how had he done it?

Daze had checked the exterior of the building, but couldn't see any way to get inside. The windows and door on the front were boarded up. A narrow path, overgrown with weeds, led around the back. There were no windows at ground level on the side of the building. The doors and windows on the back had also been boarded up. As far as I could make out, the boarding seemed to be intact; there was no obvious sign that anyone had tried to force their way inside.

I was well and truly stumped.

"What are you doing here, Jill?" I almost jumped out of my skin.

"Grandma? What are *you* doing here?"

"I asked first!" she snapped.

"I was just taking a walk when I happened to notice this old building."

"Surely by now, you must know I can tell when you're lying. I'll ask again: What are you doing here?"

It was pointless trying to pull the wool over Grandma's eyes.

"I asked Daze to follow my father."

"Why are you still wasting time on him? And what's he got to do with The Central?"

"I just wanted to know why he'd come back to Candlefield, so I asked Daze if she'd follow him for a few days. Most days he simply walks a circular route which takes him back to his flat. But on two occasions, he reached this point, and then disappeared."

"And you care why?"

"I don't. I was just curious about where he'd gone. I wanted to know how he could disappear like that."

"Do you know the history of this building?"

"Not really. Only what Daze told me. She said it used to be a meeting place for sups."

"That's only a small part of its history. The ground floor and first floor were hired out for all manner of events, but the top floor was empty for decades until Braxmore moved in. He made it his HQ."

"Who?"

"Braxmore. Probably the most evil sup there has ever been."

"I've never heard his name before."

"You won't have. These days, people are so focussed on TDO that they forget who his mentor was."

"Braxmore was TDO's mentor?"

"So the story goes, although no one knows for sure."

"What happened to Braxmore?"

"No one knows that either. He disappeared around the time that TDO came to prominence. The rumours which circulated at the time, suggested that TDO had turned on his mentor. Braxmore was never seen again."

"TDO killed him?"

"That's what we're supposed to think."

"You don't sound convinced."

"I prefer to rely on proof rather than speculation."

"Did you know Braxmore?"

"That depends what you mean by 'know'. Just like TDO, very few people actually knew him. I knew *of* him, and what I knew, I didn't care for."

"So why was The Central closed down?"

"When Braxmore disappeared, the powers-that-be took the opportunity to shut the building before a successor could take up residence. It was just the kind of cowardly decision I've come to expect from them. Instead of tackling the problem head-on, they brushed it under the carpet, and hoped it would disappear."

"That strategy doesn't appear to have worked with TDO, does it?"

"Precisely. The only way to deal with evil is to confront it."

"Why haven't they demolished the building?"

"That's a very good question. I didn't agree with its closure, but once that decision had been made, it made no sense to leave the building standing. Unless—" She hesitated.

"Unless what?"

"Never mind. Come on. It's time we were leaving."

"Hold on. What were you going to say? Unless what?"

"Unless someone gave orders to leave it standing."

"Who?"

"You ask too many questions. I don't have the time to hang around here all day."

"Why would my father come here?"

"More questions! I've no idea, but I'll wager he was up to no good."

"Do you think he found a way inside?"

"You don't actually know he went inside. You only have Daisy's word that he disappeared. He probably knew she was following him and deliberately lost her."

"But Daze is really smart!"

"So she says. Look, it's time we both got going. The less time you spend around this place, the better." She looked up at the forbidding building. "I have bad memories of this building—very bad memories."

***

I'd tried to get Grandma to elaborate on her 'bad memories' comment, but she brushed me off. She insisted I leave with her even though I'd wanted to stay and look around The Central some more. That would just have to wait for another day.

Back at my flat, I had the whole evening to myself. This was my opportunity to really study Magna's book. It took me ages to read through it, but even longer to actually understand the concepts behind it. It was way more complicated than I'd expected, but slowly and surely it all started to make sense. It was nothing like the magic that I'd been practising up until now. They were basically the same spells, but the added power and the ability to mix and match meant the possibilities were endless. It was a scary thought to have such power at my fingertips. Maybe too scary — I wasn't sure I wanted such responsibility.

I now understood why Magna had felt the need to hide the book. She'd known she was dying, and feared that, in the wrong hands, this blend of magic could do irreparable harm. What I didn't understand was why she hadn't simply destroyed the book so it would die with her. She must have hoped that one day someone would take up her mantle. She surely wouldn't have expected that someone to be a level three witch who hadn't even known she was a witch for most of her life. I didn't feel worthy to be her successor, but what choice did I have? I'd entered the sealed room, and read her book. There was no undoing that.

And why had Grandma orchestrated the whole thing so that I'd find the book? What had made her believe I would be able to get into that room? So many other witches — much more powerful than me — had tried and failed.

I felt such a weight of responsibility on my shoulders. What was I going to do? I wished Magna was still here, so that I could ask her advice. I now had great power, but what was I supposed to do with it? The obvious thing was to use it against TDO. Maybe he'd hoped to stop me before I found the book. Or maybe, he'd deliberately waited until I had the power that came from Magna's book. The more I tried to figure it out, the more confused I got.

When I'd first started out in Candlefield, I'd had Aunt Lucy and Grandma, and even the twins to talk to and ask questions. Now, there was no one I could turn to—no one at all.

I was on my own.

Chapter 21

I'd decided to give Bar Fish another try. I liked the concept, but my first visit had been tainted when I'd bumped into Alicia, who I hated with a passion. Maybe this time I'd be able to enjoy the experience.

The bar was quiet, but then it was early afternoon. I asked the bartender to choose a fishtail for me, and then found a quiet corner table. I was surrounded by fish: in the wall immediately behind me, in a large tube which ran past my table to the bar, and in the tank below my feet. It was a fantastic feeling. A bit like scuba diving, but without those stupid things you have to wear on your feet.

I'd only been there a matter of minutes when I heard a couple come in through the door. They were laughing and giggling, and generally seemed to be having a great time. To my amazement, it was Luther and Betty. He had his arm around her waist. They ordered drinks, and then took a table close to the window. They hadn't noticed me, but then I'm not sure they'd noticed anyone. They were too busy staring into each other's eyes.

Now, I know this is going to make me sound like a horrible, conceited person, but trust me on this one. Unlike me, Betty Longbottom was not in the same league as Luther Stone. Luther was an extremely handsome man with a body to die for. He oozed sex appeal, and was probably a nine if not a ten. Whereas Betty—well what can I say? Betty was just Betty. She collected crustaceans— need I say more? She was a nice enough person, or at least she was when she wasn't wearing her tax inspector's hat or attacking me with jellyfish.

So how was it that I'd spent forever trying to get a date

with Luther Stone without so much as a sniff? I'd practically thrown myself at him. On at least two occasions, I'd assumed that we were going on a date, but I'd been let down badly both times. And now, because Lucinda had given him the boot, Luther had decided that Betty Longbottom was his ideal woman. Was there no justice in the world? Why did I care anyway? I had Jack now; I didn't need Luther. And yet, it still grated.

I finished my drink, and walked nonchalantly past their table.

"Oh, hello, Luther, Betty. I didn't see you come in," I lied.

"Hi, Jill." Betty beamed. "What do you think of this place?"

"It's okay, if you like fish."

"I *do* love fish," she said. "That's why we came here. I was telling Luther about my collection of sea shells."

I expected him to laugh, but instead he said, "Betty's going to show them to me."

Yeah, I just bet she is.

"In fact," he continued. "She's more or less convinced me that I should start my own collection."

I was almost lost for words, but managed, "That sounds fascinating. I'd love to hear more, but I have to get going. Plaices to go, fish to fry."

Clearly, the universe had tilted on its axis. Instead of dressing in a sexy little black number, and using all of my feminine wiles to attract Luther, I should have just shown him a few sea shells.

***

"Quick, Jill! I need your help!" Winky was on me as soon

as I walked into my office.

"*You* need *my* help?"

"Hard to believe, I know, but this is an emergency."

"Does it involve salmon or full-cream milk?"

"Nothing so trivial. Bella has been kidnapped, or should I say, catnapped."

"Are you sure?"

"Of course I'm sure! Do you think I would joke about something like this?"

"When did it happen?"

"Yesterday."

"How do you know that she's been catnapped, and not just wandered off?"

"Bella's a top model. The catnappers must know they can get a handsome ransom for her."

"A handsome ransom?" I chuckled.

"Now is not the time for your silly jokes!"

"Sorry. Force of habit. Has there been a ransom demand?"

"Not yet."

"How did you find out about this?"

"I've been trying to get hold of her for over a day, but with no success, so I went over there."

"How did you get out of the office?"

"Never mind that. When I got to her apartment, I overheard the humans talking about her. They sounded worried, and said they had no idea where she'd gone. The woman was quite distressed."

"I still think it's possible that she's just wandered off or got lost."

"No, I'm convinced there's something sinister afoot. That's why I need your help."

"I'm not sure what I can do."

"You're a private investigator, aren't you?"

"Well, yes, but I don't normally take this kind of case."

"I'll pay you."

"What did you just say? *You'll* pay *me*?"

"Of course. On results, obviously. Provided you find her, and bring her back safely, then yes, I'll pay you a small fee."

"How small?"

"You're not going to quibble about money, are you? There's a cat's life at stake here. Will you do it or not?"

"Yes, of course. I'll get straight on it."

"Good. I'll expect an hourly report."

So, this is what my career had come to. I was now working a case for my cat.

This wasn't going to be easy. I'd spoken to Bella's owner once before, and it had been pretty embarrassing. On that occasion, it had been Bella's birthday, and I'd been delivering flowers on behalf of Winky.

I took a deep breath and knocked on the door. It took a few moments, but then a man answered.

"Hello," I said, all bright and breezy-like.

He stared at me. "Don't I know you from somewhere?"

"Me? No. I don't think so."

"I'm sure I do—I just can't think where from."

"I get that a lot. I have that kind of face."

"Wait a minute. I remember now. Didn't you bring a bunch of flowers for my cat?"

"Oh, yes. Of course. I'd completely forgotten about that."

"You said the flowers were from *your* cat."

"Winky."

"Whaty?"

"Winky? That's my cat's name. He's only got one eye."

"What brings you here today?"

"I heard that your cat has gone missing."

"How do you know that?"

That was a very good question.

"Did you take Bella?" he said, accusingly.

"Me? No! Do I look like a catnapper?"

"Possibly. You certainly have an unhealthy interest in my cat. You brought her flowers!"

"I told you. They were from Winky."

"So how did you know Bella was missing? We haven't told anyone apart from our immediate neighbours, and the police of course."

This wasn't going well.

"I—err heard from—err the police." Jack was going to kill me. "I sometimes work with them."

"What do you mean 'work with them'. What are you exactly? Some kind of cat detective?"

"No, I'm a private investigator."

"Ah, now I get it. You're an ambulance chaser!"

"No! That's not it!"

"It wouldn't surprise me if you'd had someone steal Bella just so we'd hire you to 'find' her. Is that how your little scam works? Am I supposed to give you fifty quid, so you can nip downstairs and get Bella from your buddy?"

"No! This is not a scam. I don't know anything about her disappearance!"

"You said you did."

"Only that she'd gone missing. I take it you haven't found her yet?"

"No, we haven't." He took a deep breath. "We're very worried. Are you sure you don't know where she is?"

"Positive."

"We don't know what to do. This has hit my wife really hard. She's gone to bed with a migraine."

"Have you thought of putting up posters?"

"I wouldn't know how to make them."

"If you have a photo, I can help with that."

"Would you? That's awfully kind. I'm sorry about what I said before."

"That's okay. You're upset. I understand."

"Wait there. I'll find you a photo."

Moments later, he returned with a framed photograph of the feline supermodel.

"Will this do?"

"Yes, that will be fine."

"Thanks. I don't know your name?"

"Jill. Jill Gooder."

"I'm Clive."

Just then, a woman appeared at his side. Her hair was dishevelled, and she looked as though she'd been crying.

"I thought you were having a lie down, Bonnie." Clive put his arm around the woman's shoulder.

"I heard someone at the door. Have you found her?"

"No, sorry."

"This is Jill Gooder, dear. She's going to put up posters of Bella."

Put them up? I'd only intended getting them printed.

"That's so kind of you." Bonnie gave me a hug.

Oh bum! It looked like I'd just talked myself into another job. When would I learn to keep my big mouth shut?

So, Winky had been right. Bella had disappeared. Was it really possible that she'd been catnapped? Did feline supermodels have a ransom value?

***

I could hear voices as I made my way up the stairs to the office. Someone was talking to Mrs V. As far as I was aware, I wasn't expecting anyone.

It was Armi. He had pulled up a chair next to Mrs V's desk, and she was wrapping wool around his outstretched hands. As soon as he saw me, he flinched.

"Hello there." I tried to sound friendly.

"It's all right, Armi," Mrs V said. "Jill isn't going to attack or insult you today. *Are you, Jill?*"

"No, of course not. Do I call you Joseph or Armi?"

"Everyone calls me Armi."

"Okay, Armi. Look, I'm really sorry about the other day. Mrs V has probably already told you that I'd been taking hay fever medication that didn't agree with me. I went a little doolally for a while there. I can't even remember what I said to you."

"You called me a goblin."

I very nearly laughed, but that would have been a big mistake because Mrs V had two knitting needles on the desk in front of her.

"A goblin? Did I really say that? That just shows I must have been out of it. I would never call anyone a goblin. Many other things perhaps, but never a goblin. Goodness knows, I've called your brother much worse things."

"*He* probably deserved it." Armi looked a little less worried now. "I've told Gordon he shouldn't put pressure on you to leave these premises. You were here first, after all."

"I doubt Gordon cares about that." I was slowly warming

to Armi.

"No. He's got a bee in his bonnet. Gordon is used to getting his own way."

"I can imagine." I glanced at Armi's hands. "I see Mrs V has got you earning your keep?"

"He volunteered," Mrs V said. "He has just the right size hands for it, don't you, Armi?"

He blushed.

"So, are you two like, an item?"

"Jill!" Mrs V gave me a look.

"Sorry. None of my business. I suppose I should be going through to my office?"

"Yes, I think you'd better."

Chapter 22

The last thing I felt like doing was wandering around the streets putting up posters of Bella, but what choice did I have? Bonnie and Clive were obviously devastated by the loss of their feline supermodel, and were under the impression that I'd volunteered to do the job. It had taken me almost an hour and a half to create the posters. Normally, I would have asked Mrs V to help, but she was otherwise occupied with Armi and a ball of wool.

"That's a very attractive cat," a man with more than his fair share of facial hair said.

That was typical of the comments I'd received. What a contrast to the time when I'd put up posters of Winky. Back then, I'd been accused of trying to scare young children.

"What a gorgeous cat. What do you call her?"

"She's not actually my cat. Her name's Bella."

"She looks like she should be on a catwalk."

"Have you seen her?"

"No, sorry."

"If you do, will you ring the number on the poster?"

"Is there a reward?"

Sheesh. What was wrong with people?

I covered a two-mile radius of the apartment, putting up the posters wherever I could. I'd had to put *my* phone number on them because I didn't know Bonnie and Clive's. By the time I'd finished, I was absolutely shattered. Still, it was all in a good cause. Winky would be grateful, and of course, Bonnie and Clive would be over the moon if Bella was found as a result.

When I got back to the office, Armi had gone. Mrs V was so engrossed in her Crochet Creations magazine that she barely noticed me. Winky was busy on my computer; at least he wasn't brooding over Bella.

"Guess what I've been doing?" I said.

"Sorting rubber bands? Making chains out of paper clips?"

"I've been putting up posters of your girlfriend all around the area."

"You needn't have bothered."

"Is that all the thanks I get? Do you know how long it took me?"

"Bella and I are finished."

"I thought you wanted me to find her."

"No need. I know where she is."

"You know? Then why did you let me put up all of those posters?"

"How was I supposed to know that's what you were doing?"

"Where is she? Is she back with Bonnie and Clive?"

"Who?"

"Her owners."

"Bonnie and Clive? I love it."

"Never mind that. Where is she?"

"Look." He held out his phone.

"What's that?"

"It's Instagram."

"What's Instagram?"

"Wow! What planet have you been on? Just look at the photo."

"Is that Socks with her?"

"Yes. Apparently, my darling brother called in on Bella

after I threw him out. He asked her to run away with him, and she agreed. Just like that! Can you believe it? Why would anyone in their right mind choose Socks over me?"

"It's hard to believe. I'm really sorry, Winky. I know how much Bella meant to you."

"Who? I've forgotten her already."

It was good to see him putting on such a brave face. I wasn't sure Bonnie and Clive would take it so well.

"What are you up to on my computer, anyway?"

"I'm setting up my profile."

"On what?"

"Perfect Match."

"What's that?"

"A dating site for felines."

"Oh? You mean Purr-fect. I get it. I take it you're looking for a new girlfriend then? What about Cindy?"

"I dumped her. She was too clingy."

"Can I help?"

"You? Help with dating advice?" He began to roll around the desk, laughing.

***

I didn't know what to do about Bonnie and Clive. I could hardly tell them that I'd seen an Instagram of their beloved cat with her new microlight flying boyfriend. I decided against telling them; sometimes ignorance was bliss. Hopefully, time would heal and they'd get over the loss of their beloved Bella.

With Bella accounted for, there was nothing for me to do in Washbridge, so I magicked myself to Cuppy C. The twins were, once again, beside themselves with excitement. This was becoming exhausting.

"We've got big news, Jill," Amber shouted.

"Yeah, just wait until you hear our news," Pearl said.

"Another conveyor belt? Oh, wait. I know. You're going to have a giant crane installed so customers can grab their food like in those arcade games."

"There's no need for sarcasm." Amber pouted.

"How about drones to deliver cake to the tables?"

"Now you're just being silly," Pearl said.

"Go on, then. What is it?"

"We've set a date for the wedding." Amber beamed.

"What? You and William?"

"No, *we* have set a date," Pearl said.

"You and Alan?"

They both laughed. "No. *We* as in me and Pearl."

"You're both getting married? That's great." I guess. "Who's tying the knot first?"

"Me," Amber said.

"And me," Pearl said, and they both giggled.

"Both of us. It's a double wedding."

Oh no!

"Huh? I thought you both said you'd rather die than have a double wedding?"

"We never said that!" Pearl objected.

"We would never say that!" Amber backed up her sister.

I was undecided which was worse: when the twins were at each other's throat or when they were being all buddy, buddy.

"I must have imagined it." Not!

"It'll be the biggest wedding event in Candlefield for years, and we want you to be the Maid of Honour."

Yippee!

"No, you don't. You must have lots of friends who would be better qualified to do it. What about—err—Daze?"

They looked at me like I'd lost my mind.

"Okay. Maybe not Daze, but there must be someone else."

"Are you saying you don't want to do it?" Amber looked like I'd just kicked her puppy.

"No. Of course not. It's just—"

"So, you'll do it?" Pearl said.

"Err—I." Oh bum! "Sure. I'd love to."

"Yay, we've got so much to plan," Amber said.

"Don't forget," I interrupted. "Aunt Lucy and Lester are getting married too."

"Pah! Their wedding will be nothing compared to ours."

"We want you to be our wedding planner too."

"Wedding planner? Me? What do I know about weddings?"

"You're smart and you're well-organised," Amber said.

That much was true.

"So, will you do it?" Pearl gave me those big eyes again.

"I suppose so."

"Yay!"

What could possibly go wrong?

***

I was still shell-shocked from the twin's double wedding bombshell when a young witch scurried into Cuppy C.

"Are you Jill Gooder?"

"Yes."

"This is for you." She handed me an orange envelope.

"What is it?"

But I was too late—she was already on her way out of the shop.

Inside the orange envelope was a single sheet of orange paper. It requested my presence at an Extraordinary General Meeting of the Level Six Witch Council. Today! In fact, the meeting was scheduled for one hour's time. Great! Thanks for the notice, guys! Why hadn't Grandma warned me about this? What could they possibly want me there for? I wasn't a level six witch.

Maybe the twins would have some idea what it was about.

"Hey, you two. Look what I've just received." I put the note on the counter, and they both read it. I didn't like the expressions on their faces one little bit.

"When did you get this?"

"Just now. Someone came into the shop, and handed it to me."

"This doesn't sound good," Amber said.

"They hardly ever call an Extraordinary General Meeting unless it's an emergency." Pearl looked concerned. "What have you done, Jill?"

"I haven't done anything."

And then, it clicked. This could only be about one thing: The Wand of Magna. Had word got out that I'd got inside the sealed room? I didn't see how because Grandma and me were the only people who knew.

"Are you sure?" Amber pressed.

"I haven't done anything."

"Are you going to go to the EGM?" Pearl said.

"I don't really have a choice, do I?"

My nerves were jangling by the time I arrived at the Town

Hall.

"Jill Gooder?" Someone shouted. I recognised her; she'd sat near to Grandma and me at the AGM.

Speaking of Grandma, where was she? Why wasn't she here to support me?

"Yeah, I'm Jill Gooder."

"You can come through now. We're ready for you."

Ready for me? What did that mean?

I followed her into the hall; it was full of witches—all of them level six. I glanced around the room, desperately hoping to spot Grandma, but she was nowhere to be seen.

"Please come up here, Miss Gooder," one of the women on the stage shouted. She had a face like thunder. "We have a few questions we'd like to ask you."

Once I was on the stage, I got in first. "What's this all about? Why have you called me here at such short notice?"

"All in good time. Please have a seat, Miss Gooder."

I was becoming more and more angry. Who did they think they were, ordering me about?

"It's come to our attention that someone has entered the sealed room at the museum."

I shrugged.

"And we believe *that someone* removed something from the room. Do you know anything about that?"

I wasn't sure what to do for the best. They clearly already knew I'd been in the sealed room, but should I admit it?

"I don't know what you're talking about."

A gasp went around the hall.

"Surely you're not denying that it was you who entered the sealed room, and took a book from inside there?"

"What book?"

"The book which belonged to Magna Mondale."

"I still have no idea what you're talking about."

"It's pointless to continue with these lies. We know you have the book, and unless you hand it over, we'll have no choice but to expel you from Candlefield."

"You can't do that!"

"We can expel any witch who breaks the witch code of conduct."

"What code of conduct? And what exactly does it have to say about some imaginary book?"

"I will ask you this only once. Where is the book?"

Before I could answer, the doors at the back of the hall crashed open.

"What's going on here?" Grandma shouted.

I could see her wart glowing red even from that distance.

"What's this all about?" she demanded, as she walked down the central aisle.

Every witch in the room suddenly found something interesting on her lap—no one dared to make eye contact with her.

Moments later, Grandma was on stage—nose to nose with my interrogator.

"What's going on here, Juniper?"

"You know full well, Mirabel. Someone has taken Magna's book."

"And you know that, how?"

"Well—" she stuttered.

"Have you been inside the room?"

"Well—err—no. It's sealed."

"Then how can you possibly know that anyone has been inside it? Let alone what they may or may not have taken?"

"But—"

"But nothing. Until you have proof that someone has been inside the sealed room, I suggest you keep your accusations to yourself." She turned on the audience. "And the rest of you should be ashamed of yourselves. Isn't it bad enough that we used to be persecuted by witchfinders in the human world? We can't allow that to happen here in Candlefield." She turned to me. "You, come with me."

Grandma grabbed me by the hand, and before I could say anything, she dragged me off the stage and out of the building.

"How did they find out, Grandma?" I said, once we were outside.

"I have no idea. But I intend to find out. Someone is going to suffer for this."

Chapter 23

Grandma had done her usual disappearing act after we left the EGM. I didn't want to hang around in case any of the other level six witches decided to have another go at me, so I magicked myself back to my flat in Washbridge.

I was still trying to work out what had happened. How had news of Magna's book got out? There had only been me and Grandma in the basement at the time. And, what was so urgent that it warranted calling an EGM? Magna's book was obviously a big deal, but why were they so keen for me to hand it over? Were they worried I might use it for evil? Didn't they trust me? As a 'latecomer' to witch society, I'd always felt something of an outsider, but never more so than right then.

There was a knock on the door.

I didn't want to see or talk to anyone. I just wanted to be left alone with my thoughts. It was probably Betty, in trouble with the police again, or Mr Ivers with his latest piece of movie news.

"Jill! Open up!"

It was Grandma.

"Where did you go, Grandma? I was looking for you."

"Never mind that. Where's Magna's book?" Her eyes darted left and right, trying to spot it.

"It's in my wardrobe."

"We need to get it out of here, right now."

"Why?"

"It's too dangerous for you to hold on to it. I thought we'd have more time before anyone realised it was out of the room, but word got out somehow."

"How though?"

"I don't know, and there isn't time to worry about that now. There are all kinds of rumours circulating around Candlefield. It's almost certain that TDO will have heard by now."

"What's it got to do with him?"

"Jill. You can be awfully naive sometimes. TDO became what he is by absorbing power from the most powerful sups around him. He tried to do that with your mother, but she managed to escape in time. Her power passed to you, which is why he's pursued you so relentlessly. The information in Magna's book provides a whole new level of power. Of course he wants it, and he'll do whatever he has to do, to get it."

"Where can we hide the book so that he won't find it?"

"Have you read it? Have you memorised it?"

"I've read it a number of times. I think I've digested it all."

"Let's hope so because there's no more time. We have to get rid of it permanently. It's the only way."

"I could take it into the garden and burn it?"

"Fire won't work. Nothing in nature will be able to touch the book."

"What then?"

"You need to throw it into the Dark Well."

"What's that?"

"Do you know the Black Woods?"

"Yes. I went there once when I was searching for a young girl who had supposedly gone missing."

"The Dark Well is on the north side of the Black Woods. Just follow the line of trees north; you can't miss it."

"What exactly is it?"

"It looks just like any other well, but essentially, it's the opening to a black hole. Anything that ends up in the well, disappears forever. Once the book is in there, no one will be able to get to it."

"Okay. Should we go now?"

"You'll have to do this alone."

"Why can't you come with me?"

"I have urgent matters to attend to."

"What could be more urgent than this?"

"For once in your life, will you stop asking questions? There isn't time. You're just going to have to trust me. If I could come with you, I would. You have to go right now. Get the book and go straight there. Don't let anyone or anything delay you."

"But, Grandma."

"Just do it! Now!"

And with that, she was gone.

Had I really memorised everything in the book? I thought so, but what if I was wrong? It would be too late once the book was in the Dark Well. Still, better that than let TDO get his hands on it.

I grabbed it from the wardrobe, and magicked myself over to the Black Woods. From there, I followed the line of trees north. Just as Grandma had said, the Dark Well looked just like every other well I'd ever seen. It stood in a clearing between the edge of the wood and the hills beyond.

I'd only taken a few steps towards it when suddenly, someone stepped out from behind a tree, and blocked my way. It was Ma Chivers.

"What are you doing with that book, Gooder?"

"None of your business. Get out of my way!"

"If that book is what I think it is, then it's very much my business."

"I said get out of my way."

"Do you really think I'm going to let you throw it in the Dark Well?" She took a step towards me.

What was I supposed to do now? I couldn't let her get hold of the book. Goodness knows what she might do with it, or who she might give it to. I had to get past her. I had to get the book into the well.

I tried to sidestep her, but she was very quick for a big, ugly woman. If I was going to get past her, I'd have to use magic. But Ma Chivers was a level six witch. I'd seen her do battle with Grandma, and it had been neck and neck. How was I, a mere level three witch, supposed to overcome her?

I closed my eyes, took hold of the pendant around my neck, and tried to recall everything I'd learned from Magna's book. I now knew how to put far more power into my spells, and how to mix them. But, although I understood the theory, I'd hardly had time to practise. And, I'd never had to use my new powers in anger.

None of that mattered now. I had no choice but to go for it.

I focused with every ounce of my strength, and mixed the 'power' spell with the 'vortex' spell. The result was a mini-tornado, the likes of which I'd never seen before. It hit Ma Chivers side-on, and sent her flying across the waste ground, leaving my path clear. While she was still trying to get back to her feet, I rushed over to the well, and threw the book into the void.

Ma Chivers soon recovered, and made her way over to the well.

"You'll pay for this, Gooder! Just see if you don't! Your end is nigh."

***

It was the next morning when the enormity of what had happened hit me. I was the only person who knew what had been in Magna's book. Talk about painting a target on my back.

My phone rang.

"Jack?"

"Hope I didn't wake you."

"No. I've been awake for ages. I couldn't sleep."

"Thinking about me?"

"Something like that."

"Tell me you're not doing anything tonight."

"I'm not doing anything tonight."

"Great! I've managed to snag a table for two at Romero's."

"Where?"

"You really are a philistine when it comes to food, aren't you? It's only the best Italian restaurant in all of Washbridge. Getting a table there is like winning the lottery."

"So how did you manage it?"

"One of the guys at work had booked it for himself and his wife, but she's just gone into labour four weeks early. So, what do you say? Is it a date?"

"You bet."

"Okay. See you tonight."

Jack's timing couldn't have been better. I needed something to take my mind off the goings-on in Candlefield.

"You look like the cat who got the cream," Mrs V

remarked when I arrived at the office.

"I'm going to Romero's tonight."

"Where?"

"You really should try to familiarise yourself with the better eateries in Washbridge. Romero's is the premier Italian restaurant in the city."

"With that nice detective, I assume?"

"Jack? Yes."

"Good for you. I might suggest to Armi that we try it out some time."

"How's the online dating going, Winky?"

"I've narrowed it down to a shortlist."

"How many are on there?"

"Fifteen."

"That's hardly a *short* list."

"I don't want to rush into anything. Once bitten."

"Have you arranged any dates yet?"

"I'm working on it. Anyway, what's up with you? You're obscenely bright this morning."

"Not that it's any of your business, but Jack is taking me to Romero's."

"Very nice." He nodded his approval. "Best Italian restaurant in Washbridge."

"How would you know?"

"I make it my business to keep abreast of these things. If you ever need any advice, just ask."

"Thanks. Good to know."

I sensed a chill in the air, and thought perhaps the colonel and Priscilla were back. I was ready to cover my eyes—just in case they'd forgotten to get dressed again. But no, it turned out to be my mother; I hadn't seen her for a while.

"Hi, Mum."

"Jill. How are you keeping?"

"A lot better since I got rid of your husband and his piano," I gave her a look.

"Sorry about that. I wasn't thinking. He was driving me crazy. I was trying to watch my soaps and he was playing that stupid piano. I couldn't hear myself think."

"So you thought you'd send him to play in my office?"

"Yeah. Sorry about that."

"Where is he playing now?"

"In the shed."

"Surely, you haven't banished him to the shed?"

"It was either that, or I didn't get to watch my soaps. So, in the shed he went."

"Poor old Alberto. He does play rather well, though."

"Hmm? I'm guessing he didn't tell you that he only knows two tunes?"

"No, he didn't. I just thought he was a naturally gifted piano player."

"He learned those two pieces by heart, and could play them blindfold, but give him anything else, and he hasn't got a clue. He can't actually read music."

"I see."

"Now you can understand why I wanted him out of the house. It's one thing listening to someone play the piano, but when you've heard the same two tunes a thousand times, it gets a bit old."

"I guess so. Maybe the shed *is* the best place for him. Anyway, to what do I owe the pleasure of your company?"

"I wanted to ask you a quick question."

"Sure. Fire away."

"I was just wondering. When will you and Jack be getting married?"

It was just as well I wasn't drinking when she said that because I would have spit it out.

"What? Say that again."

"You and that nice detective. I just wondered if you've set a date yet."

"No, Mum. We haven't set a date yet. We've only just started dating."

"You seem to have been seeing each other for ages."

"Professionally, yes. He works for the police, and I'm a private investigator, so our paths have crossed. But as far as being romantically involved, that's a much more recent event. We certainly haven't discussed marriage."

"You don't want to leave it too long, Jill. You're not getting any younger."

"Gee thanks, Mum. Thanks very much."

"Just look at the twins. They're younger than you, and they've both set a date."

"Ah, now I understand. That's what this is all about. You've heard about the double wedding."

"Of course I've heard about it. I believe you're going to be Maid of Honour."

"Apparently." I sighed.

"You could sound a little more enthusiastic."

"I couldn't, trust me. They want me to be their wedding planner too."

"Anyone would think you didn't like weddings, Jill."

"And, anyone would be right."

"I want to see you married. I want grandchildren."

"Hold on right there. I think we're getting a little ahead of ourselves. Firstly, Jack and I have only just started seeing each other. And, secondly, it may not last. We could very easily fall out next week; ours is a rather volatile relationship. So as for marriage and grandchildren, I wouldn't hold your breath."

"Sometimes, Jill, you disappoint me."

Chapter 24

A candlelit dinner for two. How very romantic.

Romero's restaurant was the perfect setting for our first date. Yes, I realise it wasn't actually our first *ever* date, but it somehow felt like it was. It was our first date since Drake and I had gone our separate ways, and since I'd given up all silly notions of pursuing Luther.

The décor and lighting was pure class. The music was perfect. In fact, everything about the place was fantastic. I was happy to let Jack order for both of us. It was going to be a great evening—I could feel it in my bones.

"Who would have thought you and I would end up like this," he said. "When I first came to Washbridge, I thought you were the biggest pain in the butt I'd ever met."

"Why, thank you, Mr Maxwell. That's the nicest thing you've ever said to me. But then, the feeling was mutual. If someone had told me that we'd go on a romantic date like this, I would have laughed in their face."

"Does Kathy know?"

"About us? She's sort of guessed. She keeps asking me questions. Like if I had breakfast at your place."

"And what did you tell her?"

"To mind her own business."

"You can't drive home tonight. Not after all the wine you've drunk."

"I haven't had any yet."

He filled my glass.

"You have now."

Our eyes met, and we both leaned forward. Our lips were only centimetres apart.

"Hello you two!"

"What the?"

It was Miles Best and Mindy Lowe.

"Hi, Jill. Hi, Jack." He grinned inanely. "Fancy seeing you two here."

"Fancy," I said, through gritted teeth.

"This is our favourite restaurant, isn't it, Mindy?"

"We come here all the time," she said. "Miles knows the owner."

"Oh, by the way, Jack, thanks for the endorsement," Miles said. "I'm going to have it added to our brochure."

Endorsement? I glared at Jack. Had he had the audacity to endorse Best P.I. Services?

"I've had a great idea." Miles grabbed two chairs from the next table. "Why don't we join you?"

While the waiter took Miles' and Mindy's orders, I leaned over, and whispered to Jack, "You gave him an endorsement?"

"I wouldn't call it an endorsement, exactly."

"What would you call it, then?" I couldn't hide my annoyance.

"So, Jack." Miles interrupted. "How long have you and Jill been an item?"

"We've known each other for quite a while now."

"You've got a good one there. She's magic, aren't you Jill?" He winked at me. "Not like some of the witches who might try to get their claws into you."

Hold on. Magic? Witches? What did he think he was doing?

I glared at him, but he didn't even notice.

"Have you met her cousins? The twins? What are their names, Jill?"

"Amber and Pearl."

"I don't think you've mentioned them." Jack looked at me.

"They run a cake shop." Miles was on a roll now. "You should get Jill to take you to see it. I hear their cupcakes are the second best in town."

This idiot was practically telling Jack I was a witch.

"Miles." I stood up and grabbed his arm. "Could I just have a quick word?"

I didn't give him a chance to refuse; I practically dragged him out of his seat. When we were outside the cloakroom, I pinned him to the wall.

"What are you playing at?" I had hold of his tie.

"What's the matter Jill? You look angry."

"What was all that about magic and witches?"

"Surely you can take a joke, can't you? That's all it was, I was just having a laugh."

"If you say another word about magic, witches or Candlefield, I will turn you into a cockroach, and then I'll crush you. Got it?"

***

The next morning, I was in my office flicking rubber bands at the wall, and pretending it was Miles Best. He and Mindy had completely ruined what had promised to be a perfect evening of food, drink and love. By the time we'd left the restaurant, Jack and I were both in a foul mood, and felt it better to go back to our own homes.

Kathy phoned.

"What?"

"Wow! What's up with you, grizzly pants?"

"I'm busy, Kathy. And, I'm not in the mood for your humour."

"Come down to Ever—there's something here that will cheer you up."

"Like I said, I'm busy."

"Honestly, Jill, you should come down now. You'll thank me."

"But I—"

She'd hung up. I hated it when she did that. Well, I wasn't going to bite this time. My work was too important to drop everything and go running whenever she called.

"I'm going down to Ever, Mrs V. Do you need anything?"

What? Okay, I admit it. I'm weak-willed.

"Now you mention it, I could do with adding a colour to my Everlasting Wool subscription. I've got the four-colour option at the moment, but I'm working on a project which is going to need five. The next subscription level will allow me to have seven. It's another three pounds a month, but it's probably worth it. Would you ask Kathy if she'll upgrade my subscription, and activate it immediately?"

"Of course. I'll mention it to her."

As I made my way down the road to Ever, I couldn't help but grudgingly admire Grandma's enterprise in introducing Everlasting Wool. She'd certainly spotted a gap in the market and filled it. Of course, her subscription model relied entirely on magic, which she shouldn't even have been using in Washbridge, but that aside, she was onto a winner.

As I got closer to Ever, I noticed some kind of disturbance outside the shop opposite. There were dozens of people trying to get into Best Wool, and they all looked very angry.

"What's going on across the road, Kathy?"

"That's why I wanted you to come down. Apparently the Never-ending Wool has stopped working." She chuckled. "I shouldn't laugh. Those poor sales assistants will be having a torrid time. I've been in their shoes, and it isn't fun."

"Has it stopped working for just a few people like it did with Everlasting Wool?"

"From what I can make out, it's stopped altogether."

"How did that happen?"

"I've no idea, but your grandmother seems awfully pleased about it."

"I'll bet she is. Is she in today?"

"Yeah, she's in the back."

"I suppose I ought to go say hello to her."

I left Kathy watching the carnage across the road.

"Well, well, if it isn't Washbridge's premier, private detective," Grandma said.

"You could always try being nice for a change, Grandma. After all, I am your long-lost granddaughter."

"This *is* me being nice. Now, what do you want?"

"Kathy called to tell me about Best Wool. They seem to be having a few problems."

"Are they?" She feigned surprise. "How very unfortunate for them."

"Are you behind this, Grandma?"

"How could you even suggest such a thing?"

"Easily. Have you cast a spell to stop Miles' subscription wool from working?"

"I may have; I may not have. Who knows?"

"If you have, I have only one thing to say to you."

"Yes?" Her wart was primed for action.

"Well done! Miles is due his comeuppance."

She obviously hadn't been expecting that response. "I didn't realise you had anything against Miles Best."

"The man is a parasite. He's just opened up a rival P.I. business here in Washbridge."

"I see. That young man certainly gets around, doesn't he? A cake shop, a wool shop, and now a P.I. agency. He's getting a bit too big for his boots."

Not to mention single-handedly ruining my love life.

"What will you do about the Never-ending Wool, Grandma?"

"Do about it? I won't do anything about it. My guess is that Best Wool will be out of business by this time tomorrow. Good riddance."

Remind me never to cross Grandma when it comes to business.

***

Despite Grandma's warnings, I knew I had to revisit The Central. The more I thought about it, the more it was clear to me that it was the epicentre of all that was evil in Candlefield. According to Grandma, it was where TDO had first come to prominence under his mentor, Braxmore. It also had some kind of connection to my father. According to Daze, he had simply disappeared outside that building on two separate occasions. I wouldn't rest until I'd got inside, and taken a look around. If my father really was TDO, as I suspected, then maybe this was his HQ. If I could find evidence to prove my theory, I could deal with him appropriately.

I'd decided to visit the building at night when there'd be no one around. It was more than a little spooky, but I was determined to do it. I'd already walked all around the building in daylight, so I knew there were no open doors or windows, but there had to be a way inside because I didn't believe my father had simply 'disappeared'. I was sure he'd got inside the building. The question was how?

Now that I had the power of Magna's magic, I was much better placed to find a way in. I used those new powers to cast an enhanced version of the 'listen' spell. The result was incredible. I could hear everything, and was able to focus on small areas of the building at a time. There was all manner of noises, most of which sounded like small creatures or insects. But then, I heard something which sounded like footsteps coming from the top floor of the building. The sound lasted for only a few seconds, and then fell silent.

How to get inside? On a hunch, I sent a pulse of sound towards the ground immediately in front of the building. The echo which came back was uniform for the area to the left of the door. I repeated the exercise for the right-hand side, and that's when I noticed a discrepancy. The echo there was inconsistent with the rest of the area.

But there was no obvious reason why.

I was missing something, but what? The area in front of me was covered in weeds and bushes just like the rest of the ground. So why did I get a different echo? I had to think like Magna, so I took a moment to recall her writings. One section in particular came back to me. She'd entitled it *'Everything is not what it seems'*. In that section, she'd discussed the power of permanent illusions. These were spells which created a perpetual illusion which affected everyone rather than the more temporary illusions I'd used myself. What if what I was seeing wasn't real? What if I was seeing an illusion? Only the most powerful witches or wizards could cast this kind of spell, and such spells could only be overcome by a witch or wizard who was even more powerful. It was a longshot, but nothing else made any sense.

I concentrated on the area of ground from where the inconsistent echo had emanated. The level of focus required was extremely draining, and I wouldn't be able to maintain it for long. If I *was* looking at an illusion, I'd only be able to dispel it if I was stronger than the person who originally cast that spell. What if that person was TDO? Then, I'd have no chance.

My head was beginning to throb with the effort, but then suddenly the pressure eased. When I opened my eyes, I saw a trapdoor in front of me. I'd done it—I'd dispelled the illusion.

Inside, stone steps led to darkness below. The light from my phone helped, but only a little. The basement was huge and empty. More steps at the opposite side of the room took me back up into the main building.

I was standing in the centre of a large atrium. There was very little to see on the ground floor. Just like the basement, it was empty except for a few old chairs and the remains of what had once been a wooden desk. From where I was standing, I could see all the way up to the roof which had probably once been glass, but had long since been boarded over.

Just then, I heard a noise from somewhere high in the building.

"Hello? Hello? Is someone there?"

There was no reply, but then I heard more sounds. They appeared to come from the top floor. Grandma had told me that Braxmore had occupied that floor; it was where he'd mentored TDO.

The staircase was littered with rubble, and my footsteps echoed every step of the way. If someone was there, they would definitely know I was on my way up. I had to be prepared for anything.

"Hello? Is anyone there?"

I couldn't hear anything now, so I started down the corridor. There were lots of small rooms on this level; their windows were now empty frames. When I reached the third side of the quadrangle, I came across a room with boarded-up windows. The door was locked, but was no match for my enhanced 'power' spell. It crashed to the floor, and sent dust flying everywhere. It was dark inside, so I used my phone again to provide light.

What I saw took my breath away. Two of the walls were covered in photographs; dozens of them—all of me. They'd all been taken in and around Candlefield. Someone had been following me, and judging by the images, they'd been very close by.

On the third wall, was a calendar. The date squares were blank except for one which had been highlighted by a border drawn in thick black marker. In the square, someone had written two letters in the same black marker: JG.

My initials.

The date was one week from today.

I explored the building from top to bottom for the next hour, but I found nothing else of interest. Whoever I'd heard earlier had obviously made their escape. Once I was back outside, I took a few moments to try to take in everything I'd seen. Someone was following me, and it was obvious that *that someone* planned to do me harm. But at least now, I could be on my guard because I knew precisely when they planned to strike. The problem was I still didn't know how.

Or who.

BOOKS BY ADELE ABBOTT

Witch P.I. Mysteries:
Witch Is When It All Began
Witch Is When Life Got Complicated
Witch Is When Everything Went Crazy
Witch Is When Things Fell Apart
Witch Is When The Bubble Burst
Witch Is When The Penny Dropped
Witch Is When The Floodgates Opened
Witch Is When My Heart Broke
Witch Is When I Said Goodbye
Witch Is When Stuff Got Serious
Witch Is When All Was Revealed

Coming Soon:
Witch Is Why... (the adventure continues)
Whoops! Our New Flatmate Is A Human! (see below)

AUTHOR'S WEB SITE
http:www.AdeleAbbott.com

FACEBOOK
http://www.facebook.com/AdeleAbbottAuthor

MAILING LIST
(new release notifications only)
http:/AdeleAbbott.com/adele/new-releases/

****

WHOOPS!
OUR NEW FLATMATE IS A HUMAN!

****

Charlie (a werewolf), Dorothy (a vampire) and Neil (a wizard) share a huge loft in Washbridge, but they can no longer make rent. They've been trying to find another supernatural (sup) to take the fourth bedroom for months now, but with no success. Their landlord is tired of waiting for his money so takes matters into his own hands, and finds them a new flatmate.

Susan Hall is an investigative reporter who has just joined The Bugle. She is ambitious, and determined to clean up the paper's sleazy image with hard hitting stories. She's been living out of a suitcase in a crummy hotel for weeks, so is delighted to be offered a flat share in a beautiful loft space.

The three original flatmates are horrified. It's bad enough that their new flatmate is a reporter, but what's even worse: she's human.

39286874R00140

Made in the USA
San Bernardino, CA
22 September 2016